KILL 'EM
WITH
KINDNESS

THE AUTHOR

KILL 'EM WITH KINDNESS

FRED DICKENSON

COACHWHIP PUBLICATIONS

Greenville, Ohio

FOR PEG

To whom Bill Shakespeare was
not alluding when he wrote—

"And if she chance to nod, I'll rail
and brawl,
And with the clamour keep her still
awake.
This is a way to kill a wife with kindness . . ."

The Taming of the Shrew
Act IV, Scene I

Kill 'Em With Kindness, by Fred Dickenson
© 2018 Coachwhip Publications

Fred Dickenson (1909-1986)
First published 1950.
No claims made on public domain material.

CoachwhipBooks.com

ISBN 1-61646-446-1
ISBN-13 978-1-61646-446-2

1
OFTEN A BRIDEGROOM

"That's my next-to-the-last duchess painted on the wall," McGann's host said. His laugh matched the black velvet of the hangings, blended with and disappeared into the lush folds lining the gallery.

Detective Mack McGann gazed raptly at the painting which glowed under artful lights. The sixth wife of Ronald Tompkins had been a haughty redhead. Tough as a ten-day eviction notice, McGann decided. She stared imperiously down from the wall, assaying her worshipers from behind the formidable bulwark of her snowy breast.

"A lovely child, Mr. Tompkins," McGann said. What the hell, he thought, there is no sense in antagonizing ten million dollars. Anyway he admired the way the swell slid gracefully into a purple cleft. "A delicate flower," he added cautiously, "too frail, perhaps, for this world."

The sleek head bobbed briefly. "She was completely out of it. Utterly."

McGann stopped admiring the bosomy beauty long enough to turn his gaze upon the man whose summons had brought him to this strange mansion in Manhattan's upper 60's. He had heard of Ronnie Tompkins and the playboy's matrimonial escapades for

years. Now the call from a client of such magnitude had left him
pleasantly dazzled.

McGann had hastened to answer the summons. But the client had shown no similar urge to unburden himself. Instead, he
personally had met the detective at the door, had guided him
through gloomy dens and hallways, and now seemed determined
to parade his gallery of glamour.

The clever lights brought the portraits to life but left the rest
of the room in heavy shadow. McGann could be certain only of
the brilliant shirt front of his tuxedoed guide, the sheen of dark,
well-brushed hair, the flash of a ring. He returned to contemplation of the glorious redhead.

"Leopold Seyffert," he said.

"I beg your pardon?"

"Seyffert. I was looking at those colors. Handled a case once
in a place that had several of his portraits."

"I see," the smooth voice dismissed his observation, concentrated on the subject. "When I found her she was Shirley Stanton,
cigarette girl at The Diamond Corkscrew. I proposed instantly.
We drove to Jersey and were married between the midnight and
two o'clock shows."

McGann nodded. "I remember," he lied. He felt he ought
to offer something more. "Country driving is nice at that hour.
Bracing."

"We were back in time for the last floor show." The voice
was triumphant. "I put her on the Century for Chicago and
Reno that afternoon. The entire marriage lasted less than sixteen
hours. I settled two hundred and fifty thousand dollars on her."

Figures flashed through McGann's mind like jet-propelled
boxcars. If Mrs. Tompkins No. 6 had been worth . . . umm . . .
roughly $15,000 an hour, there was no telling what a top-flight
private investigator might rate.

He had been on this job for fifteen minutes. Technically he could already have earned $3,500 plus, if scaled no higher than New York's most enchanting cigarette girl. The possibilities were staggering. He said enthusiastically, "It's all terribly interesting, Mr. Tompkins."

McGann was rewarded with a murmur of pleasure. They turned to the portrait of Kathleen Rogers, Wife No. 5. She had big sad eyes and bluish hair. McGann recognized Alexander Brook in the harmony and close values; financially Tompkins had gone all out on his gallery. The voice oozed from the shadows behind him, "Only society girl I ever married. It was a mistake, of course."

In quick succession they surveyed a row of stunning blondes, Wives I through IV inclusive. "My platinum period," the host chuckled. He ticked them off. "Gladys Mars, Number One, from the chorus of 'Down The Hatch.' Hope Harmon, you remember her specialty in 'Two's Company'? Faith Starr—she had the lead in 'The Purple Pigeon'—it laid an egg, too. Irma Nelson, head waitress at Hamburger Heaven."

"Terrific," McGann said reverently. "Every one a collector's item."

They stopped before a covered easel. There seemed to be a new quality in the unctuous voice now. Did the white hand tremble a trifle as it touched the cord? He said, "I hope it isn't bad luck, but I decided to have this portrait painted before the ceremony."

"Mrs. Tompkins the Seventh?" asked McGann brightly.

The dinner jacket tilted in a slight bow. "Exactly. My lifetime ambition; my ultimate goal. My seventh wife and the most beautiful girl in the world."

He pulled the cord and the silk covering whispered back. McGann saw the truly lovely face of a dark-haired girl. Her deep-set eyes were an odd green-brown; her lips were full and curved in the faintest of smiles. He experienced a curious feeling that they had met.

His host's next words solved the mystery. "Charity Jones, the model," he said. "It isn't her real name, of course. Just something Harry Conover hung on her. But fitting, don't you think?"

"Yes. Yes, indeed," McGann said.

The voice warmed. "It got so that I was seeing her face everywhere. If I shopped for bracelets or furs—Chary was modeling them and always appearing prettier than the girl I was escorting." He sighed. "Naturally, I couldn't have that."

"Sooner death," McGann said.

"When I learned that she was called 'Charity' Jones, I felt that it was definitely an omen. I already had married Faith and Hope. This will complete the picture, in all ways."

McGann resisted a strong impulse to pinch himself. The setting was the most fantastic of his career. Nothing had approached it during his years with the FBI. The cases he'd had since opening a private agency in New York City had been conventional by comparison.

He had solved the mystery of the disappearing merchandise in the shipping department of an uptown store—simply by determining which stock clerk was driving the biggest car. Later, a wealthy Long Island client had been grateful to discover through McGann that his prospective son-in-law once had been a leader of the younger set at Dannemora. But competition was keen. Sometimes, McGann thought ruefully, there seemed to be ten investigators for every mystery. The call half an hour before from the home of the fabulous Ronnie Tompkins had come like a bid to a rummage sale at Fort Knox.

Yes, it was undeniably true that Tompkins, whose millions flowed from Chilean copper mines, had married six breathlessly beautiful girls and now was intent upon marrying the seventh and loveliest.

Everyone knew all about it. Vivid accounts had appeared in the *News* and in the *Mirror* and had been corroborated by a paragraph on Page 22 of *The Times*. Ronnie Tompkins existed and McGann was looking at the newly-finished portrait of the girl who would be Mrs. Tompkins No. 7.

He wondered what you say to a man—a multimillionaire client—who shows you the picture of his seventh bride-elect. He decided to play it safe. "An angel on leave," he said.

With infinite tenderness, the covering was slipped back over the perfect features. The press of a wall switch dimmed the lamps, leaving a single tiny vigil light in the gallery of the gorgeous.

"Please come into the study; I'll mix you a drink." Apparently it was felt that some explanation was needed for this manual labor. "I gave the servants the rest of the evening off. They can't seem to resist eavesdropping."

Incredible carpets hushed their footfalls. A cheerful fire crackled on the hearth against the sharp fall evening. McGann caught a glimpse of gleaming andirons. Appreciatively, he sniffed an atmosphere that was a heady compound of leather, well-rubbed furniture and burning hardwood. He was waved to a chair beneath the only light that was on.

In a few moments he felt comfortably relaxed. The monogrammed cigarette was well blended, the Scotch was properly ancient. He sipped the dry cool drink, pulled on the cigarette and waited.

His host was out of the circle of light so that McGann, sitting almost directly under it, could hardly see him. McGann was familiar with the trick, which reminded him of an FBI grilling—certainly he himself had employed it often enough—but he was content not to do anything about it at the moment. In fact, he was regretful when, at last, the voice began on the business at hand.

"You are wondering why I called you?"

Here it comes, McGann thought. Get enough on some girl to stop incipient blackmail. Follow the butler and see if he isn't betting the knives and forks in a floating crap game. He said, "Wondering but not worried, Mr. Tompkins. This is a pleasant way to work."

There was a brief silence. Then, "Two years ago, you headed a Federal squad which broke up an international swindle ring operating out of El Paso, correct?"

"Correct."

"That was of direct benefit to a company in which I am an important stockholder. Your role did not go unnoticed."

McGann allowed his hopes to rise higher. Mentally, he dismissed the gambling butler and girded to battle the mysterious account juggling which was plaguing the Tompkins empire.

"You are well known among New York police and friendly with top officials?"

"I know them," McGann admitted. "And we're certainly chummier since they don't think my appearance means Washington is trying to steal their thunder."

The dinner jacket blurred forward, a tiny rainbow flicked from the diamond on the suddenly raised hand. "Excellent, Mr. McGann. You are just the man I want to prevent a case."

McGann swallowed. "You want me to prevent a case? Don't you mean solve?"

"I mean exactly what I said."

The detective carefully tapped his cigarette ash into the tray. All right—so Ronnie Tompkins was getting to the point where he talked in riddles. He could go along with the gag. It seemed better not to press the point. He smiled encouragingly. "What's the case, Mr. Tompkins?"

With a muted crash one of the logs broke and fell. Sparks showered upward, and a red whip of light lashed the ceiling. The voice had lost none of its smooth calm as it gave an answer which made McGann stiffen in his chair.

"My murder," he said.

2

STONE COLD DEAD IN THE P.M.

The words "My murder" vibrated in the shadowy study. McGann glanced suspiciously at the half empty glass of Scotch and soda which was coolly golden in his hand. It was good but not that good. He had heard correctly.

He said, "Suppose you tell me why you expect to be murdered, Mr. Tompkins." The lamplight in his eyes was beginning to annoy him. Multimillionaire or not, he would put up with these cute eccentricities just so long. "Have you been threatened?"

The detective's host was a black and white smudge behind the desk. Now he began to talk and as the voice droned on, McGann understood many things he had overlooked in his heretofore light perusal of Ronnie Tompkins' marriage marathon.

"In the course of marrying six beautiful girls and wooing a seventh, a man is virtually certain to make deadly enemies, wouldn't you say?"

McGann winced. "It's a lot of mothers-in-law," he admitted.

"Many deadly enemies." The voice took on a dreamy quality, soothing above the soft whisper of the fire. "Some of my brides, for instance, have not particularly welcomed my suggestion that they rush to Reno before the rice has stopped bounding. They seem to feel, somehow, that I am criticizing them personally."

McGann nodded.

"They have not fully grasped the meaning of my proposals. Each one appears to think that for some strange reason I shall want to settle down with her when I never wanted to do so with anyone else. This is a display of egoism which I find particularly obnoxious." The diamond flashed again as the hand came up and touched the perfect tie.

"My great-grandfather cheated me, Mr. McGann. He made a million dollars which my grandfather foolishly allowed to grow into three million. My father completed the damage by doubling this ridiculous fortune and passing on to me six million dollars. By its own sheer force it has swelled to ten million dollars. You can imagine what that sum does to all worthwhile ambition."

McGann grinned. "It would satisfy mine."

The voice turned sharp. "You are guilty of the usual crude observation. Believe me, it is not amusing. I have always been denied what I am sure must be a man's greatest satisfaction—the proving of his worth to the world.

"Instead, somehow, I wasted years in nebulous pursuits and then launched upon my series of marriages. I don't believe I thought of it as a life's work until after the third. I had, of course, read the life of Henry the Eighth and noted that he had six wives. I felt that I could do better and have all of them true beauties besides.

"Now I am ready to set the new mark. But my enemies are growing more numerous and threatening."

McGann nodded. "You mean some of the boys you and the Tompkins bankroll outweighed?"

His host's cigarette glowed. "The world has stubbornly refused to understand my motives and give me the credit to which I feel entitled. Let us take the case of the last Mrs. Tompkins.

I find a vision of loveliness forced by circumstances to peddle cigarettes to a den of jackasses. I marry her—approach one bride closer to my goal—and hand her two hundred and fifty thousand dollars to go and divorce me, in addition to all expenses.

"I am amused. The girl is freed of the lowliest servitude. I have struck a blow for beauty."

"And her boyfriend burns."

The diamond glittered in a disdainful gesture. "I have never fully understood why the loveliest girls seem to favor an especially unprepossessing type of heel. Watch for it and you will see what I mean.

"Show me a pretty girl from the village to Fifty-Second Street and nine times out of ten I will show you a lowbrow sharpie at her elbow. The traditionally heroic type couldn't afford to take her out."

McGann shifted. "That's me," he said, "the heroic homebody. Just a parlor playboy." He rose suddenly and stepped outside the circle of light. "Mind if I strengthen this ice?"

The abrupt change blinded him temporarily. As his vision cleared, his host was mopping his forehead. "Not at all. None for me, thanks. I'm all caught up." When McGann was seated again the subject was pressed afresh.

"The other night, as I crossed the street at the corner down here, a car swerved and narrowly missed me. At first I put it down to the usual stupid driving of anyone out after two A.M."

McGann took a small notebook from his inside breast pocket and noted the date, Friday, Oct. 10. "Just exactly when was that, Mr. Tompkins?"

"It was—ah—Tuesday morning. A bit after two. Say ten after. I was home early, taking a little stroll before retiring."

"Then that's not a customary time for you to be around the neighborhood on foot?"

"No."

"Go on."

"Last night, I am sure that I was followed. A short thickset man and a blackhaired girl appeared in three nightclubs—the Stork, Ruban Bleu and Cafe Society Uptown, coming in always a few minutes after my party was seated."

"Ever see them before?"

"No. They are not what you would call pub-crawlers of major league calibre or I should have recognized them. Today, I believe I saw the woman in the neighborhood."

McGann dutifully wrote it down. He masked a growing disappointment. These seemed the flimsy suspicions of a wealthy neurotic, wraithlike fears which stalked a champagne-soaked brain. What Ronnie Tompkins wanted was a bodyguard, a brass-knuckled character with a pistol permit. But he decided to probe a bit deeper before bowing out.

"Anything more concrete, Mr. Tompkins?"

"Yes. In addition to these other things which I have mentioned, something occurred late this afternoon which made me decide to call you. I received a personal warning."

McGann's interest brightened perceptibly. "Who from?"

"Frazier Farwell." The name was familiar to McGann but nevertheless he wrote it down. "He's a record player on an after-midnight radio program. The 'Can You Imagine Ballroom' or some such."

"I've heard of him," McGann said. "He's one of our better disc jockeys as we say around the soda fountain. He grooves a drastic plastic."

The dim figure leaned back in the vast leather chair. "I am not prepared to evaluate his contribution to the airwaves. It will be up to you to evaluate his contribution to the matter at hand."

McGann jotted briefly as the recent role of the radio performer was unfolded. Farwell was just one of many minor celebrities, who over the years had attached themselves to the tail of the Tompkins' comet. Sometimes he joined a Tompkins' party at a nightclub, where nobody ever had been known to wrest the check from the host.

Farwell paid for this regular free-loading by dedicating radio numbers to Ronnie Tompkins and his bride of the moment. It was all good clean fun and wholesome publicity. He usually played a few turns of Mendelssohn's wedding march, followed by Guy Lombardo's Decca platter of "After You've Gone." Nobody took offense.

McGann asked, "How did Farwell warn you?"

"He came here. He's here now. He was quite drunk and I put him to bed upstairs. My first impulse was to throw him out but in a way I've always been fond of Frazier. He's so good-natured about being a failure."

"But he said something which made you change your mind?"

"Yes. He was hardly coherent and I was inclined to believe it was only the liquor talking. It seems that somebody had approached him for information about me—somebody who couldn't possibly want it for any good. I was ready to dismiss it. Then I thought of the other incidents of which I've told you and made up my mind to investigate the whole business.

"He's been sleeping for a couple of hours now and it should be possible to get some sense out of him. I wish you'd go up and talk to him."

McGann slipped the notebook into his breast pocket. "All right, Mr. Tompkins, I'll see him. Where is he?"

"You'll find him in the rear bedroom on the third floor. Go right in. The house is yours, Mr. McGann. Meanwhile I have a few things to do here before going out to dinner—" He laughed softly. "I think I'll be safe."

McGann rose. He was glad to get out of the strong light of the lamp. He turned at the door leading into the hallway and said, "I'd rather you didn't leave the house, though, until I come back. In fact, it wouldn't do any harm to lock this door. At least until we find out what's bothering Farwell."

"I'll take care of it."

McGann stepped into the hallway, closing the door to Tompkins' study behind him. The same thick carpeting yielded beneath his feet as he moved cautiously toward the front door where a great staircase curved upward into the shadows.

On the wall, a small orange bulb fought a losing battle with the corridor's gloom. McGann picked his way carefully. Whatever Ronnie Tompkins' extravagances, subsidizing the Edison Company was not one of them. Here, he supposed, Tompkins counter-balanced the bright study light.

Behind him, McGann heard the lock click on the study door. He paused near the front entrance. His hat and coat lay on a chair there. For a moment, he toyed with the alluring idea of picking them up and walking out.

Eccentric millionaires rarely were worth the trouble they caused their employees, he reflected. For a thousand dollar retainer you drew ten thousand dollars worth of headaches.

On the other hand, Ronnie Tompkins could be a highly desirable client. And thus far, certainly, McGann had not been imposed upon. He came out of his reverie, with reluctance passed up the hat and coat, and put a foot on the first heavily-carpeted step.

There was a sudden excited whir from the corner. McGann's gaze flicked round and he laughed shortly as a towering grandfather clock struck a solemn half hour. Automatically he checked it with his wrist-watch—6:30 P.M.

The big old house was heavy with smothering silence when the chime died away. Places like this, throwbacks to the stately days of the brownstones, always depressed McGann. Most of the homes by this time had been cut up into light-housekeeping rooms where radios blared and cabbage was king. This one, through a combination of money and the idiosyncrasies of its owner, had been retained in all of its original charm.

Still it weighed upon his spirits. Now, as he stood listening, his ears became better attuned to the place. There were distant creakings, inescapable in subway-laced Manhattan. A flurry of car honkings, filtering through the thick walls, drowned what might have been a door closing.

Slowly, McGann started up. It was typical of wealthy and spoiled playboys like Ronnie Tompkins that he should be told to go and find Farwell. A client less well-to-do probably would have led the way personally.

Halfway to the second floor, there was a niche in the wall off the left-hand side of the staircase. A bronze nude reposed there, gazing languidly upward at a tiny bunch of bronze grapes. His progress muffled, McGann rose past the shadowy statue.

The second-floor hallway was almost pitch dark. He allowed his fingers to trail lightly along the silky balustrade. It guided him to the clock-wise circling bannister which swooped upward to the third floor.

"They should send a stewardess with you on this trip," McGann muttered as he moved higher. His eyes were becoming used to the gloom now and he could see well enough. The second staircase was more utilitarian and less decorative than the one below. It boasted no bronze nude in a niche.

McGann looked about when he achieved the third floor landing. The rear of the house would be to his left and the bedroom there could be only on one side. It should be a simple matter now to locate the platter turner rendered *hors de combat* and discover what he knew, if anything

McGann was surprised to see a thin slash of light at the bottom of the door to the rear bedroom where he had been told

Frazier Farwell could be found. He had expected the place to be dark, his quarry snoring in an alcoholic coma. The surprising light led him to eschew the knob and to rap sharply instead.

The sound reverberated in the close confines of the upper corridor. McGann waited. There was no answer. He placed his ear to the door but could hear nothing. What was it that he had been told? "The house is yours." He turned the knob and pushed. The door was locked. The keyhole was black.

Uncertainly, McGann stepped back. He peered over the railing. The steps fell away rapidly into the gloom below. He thought: It's a long way down for another key, even if I can push out the one that's already there.

Was Farwell sleeping with the light on? Or had he awakened and gone to a bathroom where he could not hear McGann's knock? The detective waited a few minutes and then again approached the door.

This time he pounded heavily. "Open up," he called. Drunks and locks were a dangerous combination. Inebriates who did not appear capable of twitching an eyebrow somehow could always manage to stagger around and lock themselves in, McGann had found. This was particularly true in relation to bathrooms. To make a lush completely happy, he thought darkly, give him a john to barricade himself in.

He pounded and listened, repeated the process. At last, his ear pressed to the door, he thought he heard water running Yes, now there was the sound of splashing. McGann turned around and used his heel. He was finally rewarded with the soft whisper of approaching footsteps.

The lock clicked back, and the door was thrown open. A pale figure swayed in the light. The man was barefoot, and he wore only a pair of violent red-striped shorts. His smooth yellow hair was dripping, and water ran down his bare chest among the thin golden hairs.

His voice was hoarse. "Please," he croaked. "You don't know what that pounding does to me. You can come in but only if you promise not to pound on anything."

McGann stepped in. Frazier Farwell's eyes were laced with angry red veins. He burped profoundly, and McGann was swept by a cloud of inferior rye.

The man apparently saw him shudder. "Sorry," he rasped. "Farwell's disease." He turned abruptly and moved toward the bathroom which opened off the far end of the room. He gestured over his shoulder. "Sit down. Make y'self to home."

McGann ignored the offer to sit down and instead followed Farwell to the door of the bathroom. The radio actor had filled the washbowl with water, and was busy ducking his head. The yellow hair came up plastered over his forehead.

"Chinese water torture," he explained. "Cures worst cases. I've been given up by three doctors and two undertakers."

"Don't drown yourself," McGann said. "At least, not yet. I'm a detective. I want to ask you a few questions."

"Oh, oh." Farwell swung about, and dripped briskly on the green tile. The bloodshot eyes widened in wonder. "A seeing eye, eh?"

"Private eye," McGann grinned. "I'm only a seeing eye from nine to five. Then I slip the leash. I hear you've been telling Ronnie Tompkins things that have got him nervous."

Frazier Farwell buried his face in a thick towel. He rubbed his head briskly, and wiped his thin shoulders and chest. "Seems to me I do remember something about that," he said evasively. "It was just before they slipped me the poisoned lemon peel."

McGann held out a pack of cigarettes. Farwell took one with trembling fingers. He produced a comb from the back pocket of a pair of slacks thrown over a chair and ran it through his butter-colored hair. Then he drew in gratefully as McGann held a match.

"I hope you can remember everything," McGann said. He shook out the match. "Tompkins said someone had been asking you questions about him."

Farwell inhaled deeply, blew the smoke out in a thin gray stream. "Oh, yeah," he said. "I—"

From below them came the crash of an exploding pistol. The crack was muffled but unmistakable in the silent house. The sound quivered on the heavy air, echoing faintly along the gloomy corridors. For a split-second, McGann stood with the burnt match in his raised fist. Farwell's hand jerked nervously.

Then McGann was out of Farwell's room and taking the steps down three at a time. Behind him pattered the radio man, also galvanized into action. Rounding the second-floor turn, McGann caught a glimpse of the red-striped shorts. Farwell had the towel over his shoulders.

The detective whirled around the newel post on the first floor, hurled himself at the door of the study. It was locked. "Mr. Tompkins!" he shouted. He rattled the knob, pounded with dosed fist. There was no answer from the room.

Farwell came panting up. "Look out," McGann said roughly. He backed up and threw 175 well-knit pounds at the door. It cracked sharply but held. McGann leaped back. Again his left shoulder crashed against the weakened wood. It splintered and flew inward, dropping the detective to hands and knees.

McGann froze halfway up. Directly ahead of him, Ronnie Tompkins lay on his back on the floor. His eyes were open, and he looked surprised. His head rested on a dainty, lace-edged pillow. His hands were at his sides, and the firelight played with the brilliant diamond.

He was dead.

3
MY HATE LIES SLEEPING

Slowly, McGann straightened. He heard Farwell behind him make a strangled noise and instinctively he held up a hand.

"Don't come in here," he said. "Don't touch anything."

Looking at Ronnie Tompkins' already waxlike features, Mc-Gann was swept with a feeling of mingled surprise and regret. Truthfully, he had not believed the man to be in any immediate danger. The reasons that had been advanced to him for fearing an attack had been thin as mist. Still, he had been appealed to, the responsibility was his—

And Ronnie Tompkins was dead.

Looking at the rug cautiously before planting a foot, McGann advanced further into the room. The acrid odor of gun-powder hung in the air. He could see a crimson stain oozing from beneath the supine figure.

A movement at the window made him swing quickly around. It was the heavy drape swaying in a sudden breeze. McGann stepped over, found himself looking out of an open window.

In the doorway, Farwell drew the towel more closely about his shoulders. He seemed completely sobered. "Be careful," he chattered.

"Sure," McGann said. Without touching the sill, he leaned out as far as he could. Directly outside the window was an iron fire-escape landing. Looking up he saw nothing but a handful of stars framed in the rectangle formed by the surrounding buildings. The counter-balanced steps were up, parallel with the landing but that did not prove that they had not recently been down.

Below was a cement courtyard lighted only by a small bulb above the rear service door of the adjoining apartment building. McGann could see nobody moving about. Several rear windows of the apartment building on the next street were lighted. One went out as he watched.

He pulled his head back in. The breeze shoved the drape again and something glinted on the floor beneath the moving hem. McGann bent over, peering practically into the muzzle of a blue-steel automatic. It looked like a .32 calibre. He wanted badly to pick it up for a closer inspection but restrained himself. His position already was sufficiently embarrassing without possibly putting fingerprints on the murder gun.

Again his gaze roamed the room. A tiny gleam near the wall took him in that direction and he saw a discharged shell such as would be ejected by the automatic. That was all that he could find. The sleek head of Ronnie Tompkins was on the little lace-edged pillow. He did not remember having seen the pillow on his previous time in the room but then he hadn't seen very much anyway. Besides the body, there was the thin, rapidly-disappearing blue smoke of exploded gunpowder, the open window and the gun.

On the burnished mahogany table next to the chair in which McGann had sat for his talk just a few minutes before were the ashtray containing the cigarette he had crushed out, and the tall, thin glass which had held his Scotch and soda. There was now only half an inch of melted ice in it.

The door leaned inward at a rakish angle where McGann's battering-ram attack had twisted the upper hinge. A subdued hissing issued from the fireplace where the remnants of the logs glowed dully.

Frazier Farwell hopped from one bare foot to the other and began to shiver in earnest, either from excitement, cold or a combination of both.

"Well, we're certainly too late to help him now," McGann said. "You'd better go up and get some clothes on."

Farwell stared. "Alone?"

"I can't leave here," McGann said patiently.

Slowly, the red-striped shorts disappeared into the hallway gloom. McGann heard him start up the stairs. For a moment, he again surveyed the room.

Of course it could have happened in any of several ways, he thought. A killer might have been hidden in the room all of the time that they had been talking. The draperies of the adjoining art gallery afforded excellent hiding places. Then about the time that McGann had begun to question Farwell upstairs there could have been a quick step out . . . the crash of gunfire . . . and flight from the window to avoid the detective who must come down the staircase.

Someone could even have climbed the fire escape, raising the window to prevent possible deflection of the bullet . . . McGann's gaze found the buzzer—had Tompkins admitted a caller while he was upstairs—a caller who followed Tompkins into the study and fired while the host's back still was turned?

McGann frowned and stepped between the body and the window. Was there still another possibility? These were precious moments when he could be alone before taking the next and necessary step. No, Tompkins never could have shot himself, staged this macabre hoax as a farewell gesture to a not too friendly world.

In the first place, judging from the spreading crimson stain, he had been shot in the back. It is difficult but not impossible for a man to shoot himself in the back. What was impossible was for a man to so shoot himself, hurl the gun a good ten feet and then stretch out to die with his head on a lace-edged pillow.

Why the pillow? McGann wondered. That was a dame's trick. Kill a guy in a burst of passion and then with a sudden rush of kindness shove a pillow under his head. Yes, that was definitely the sort of thing you might expect a woman to do.

Still, he had known male killers who perpetrated terrible crimes and then stacked the girl's clothes neatly, garments folded and shoes precisely side by side. That was the kind of psychological quirk that fictioneers laid off of. But there were countless records in police files . . .

The word "police" itself brought him back to action. He had been a Federal officer for so long that he had almost forgotten that he was now a private agent with definite responsibilities to the constituted authorities.

McGann took a white handkerchief from the breast pocket of his suit and stepped to the telephone which was on Ronnie Tompkins' desk. He used the handkerchief to lift the instrument, and when he heard the dial tone he took the pencil from his vest pocket and dialed SPring 7-3100. When the operator answered at police headquarters, McGann asked for Homicide. He gave them the address and the information that Ronald Tompkins had been shot and was dead.

"Who's this?" Homicide asked. McGann told them. "Stay there," the voice said. "We'll be right over."

McGann replaced the instrument. He moved carefully around the body, and headed for the hall to wait there. Now he did not even want to sit in the room or disturb it in any way. He had used the telephone there because he did not want to leave the place unguarded. But he had distributed no extra fingerprints.

He looked up as the doorbell rang. It was just the buzzer in the study, apparently one that could be thrown on when servants were out, but the summons was unexpected.

"Now they're not *that* fast," McGann muttered. He again brought out the handkerchief as he strode swiftly to the front door and he used it to turn the knob. A girl stood on the threshold; a very pretty girl.

"Oh," she said, seeing McGann. "I'm sorry." She stepped back, seemingly puzzled, and looked at the number above the door. McGann noticed that her dark brown hair gleamed warmly. A green cloth coat hung from her shoulders and a hatbox dangled by a ribbon from her arm.

Her puzzlement appeared to increase after a second glance from the house numeral to the detective.

"This is Mr. Tompkins' home, isn't it?" she asked. Her voice was friendly but firm. She looked full at McGann and now he could be certain that her eyes were that odd blend of green and brown. He recognized Charity Jones, the model, the girl who now would never be Mrs. Tompkins No. 7.

"Yes, it is," he said. He hesitated. Did he want this girl to be there when police raced up or didn't he? There was no more than half a minute to decide.

"Well?" She looked half annoyed, half puzzled, as if trying to determine whether McGann were a butler in mufti or an especially insouciant housebreaker. She gestured with graceful hands in white knit gloves.

"Please tell Mr. Tompkins that Miss Jones is here." She made as if to enter, glanced up with controlled but rising indignation as he continued to block the entrance.

"Listen." McGann bent forward suddenly. From far off he had heard the first thin scream of a police siren. Within seconds now, he knew, the cars would turn the corner. Uniformed figures and plainclothesmen would leap out, flashlights would stab the darkness, photographers' bulbs would wink brightly. He began to speak rapidly. "My name's Mack McGann and I'm a private detective. Mr. Tompkins has met with a serious accident. Police are on their way here now . . ."

She stared as if he suddenly had loosed a flood of a little-known Mongolian dialect.

"You'd better not be found here." The siren was louder, closer, the advance agent of a blinding spotlight of publicity, suspicion. Had the girl just happened by at this inopportune time or was there reason for her presence? How long would it take a person to go down the back fire-escape, walk through the service corridor of the apartment building next door and ring the Tompkins front entrance buzzer as if nothing had happened?

"This is for your own good," McGann said. "Don't go home, either. Go to the movies, anywhere. Meet me at the fountain at the Fifty-Ninth Street plaza at ten o'clock." His voice rose. "Don't stand there, damn it! Get going!"

Chary Jones whirled. He had a flash of nice legs and well-shaped ankles above sling-back sandals. She flicked down the brownstone steps and disappeared westward toward Fifth Avenue and Central Park. The siren filled the night now and the leading headlights stabbed around the corner.

McGann closed the door quickly and stepped back. A moment ago, he had been congratulating himself upon the eminently fair way in which he had handled matters. He had touched nothing, interfered not at all and promptly had notified the New York City police that they had a hell of a murder on their hands.

This was against every natural impulse. During his years as a Federal agent, he usually had found himself working against local police or at least independent of them. There was a good deal more rivalry between city authorities and G-men than the general public realized.

Now at the very last instant, McGann had tampered with the natural course of events. He had advised Chary Jones to keep moving. Why? Half-regretfully, he hoped that it was because he did not wish to stand idly by and see a nice girl blunder into a top role in a murder investigation. Which was exactly what would have happened had he allowed her to step inside. Yes, that was why he had told Miss Jones to hit the road and not for home, either. They'd look for her *there* in a hurry. He'd wanted to give her a chance to keep her pretty little nose clean . . . he wanted to talk to her before anybody else did.

It was not, he assured himself, so that he could enjoy one bit of information the investigating officers would not know. Certainly not. A charge as false as it was malicious. . . .

The front door practically jumped into the hallway under the crash of official fists. McGann took a deep breath. "J. Edgar Hoover be with me," he said, and opened it.

4

BRING OUT YOUR RUBBER-TIRED CARRIAGE

Deputy Chief Inspector Cornelius Patrick O'Callahan peered out from beneath jutting brows that were like white cotton tufts pasted on a block of pink wood. He drummed with heavy square fingers on the desk of the late Ronnie Tompkins.

"The deceased," he asked McGann again, "mentioned no names?"

"No names, Inspector," McGann said for the seventh time. He heard the clock in the front hall chime the half hour and he looked at his watch—9:30. For almost three hours, this had been going on.

O'Callahan and his men had clamped a steel grip on the Tompkins residence within minutes of their arrival. Men had deployed everywhere with remarkable speed. Already, one had struck his head smartly on a basement girder, and a colleague had twisted his ankle on the roof.

But these minor mishaps detracted not a bit from a smooth display of efficiency.

The official police photographers had photographed the body from at least nine different angles. Fingerprint men had dusted every conceivable surface of the study and adjoining art gallery. One had picked up the pistol near the open window by inserting a thin steel rod into the barrel, not touching the weapon itself with his hands. He had snared the ejected shell in the same way.

When the print men had finished with them, the pistol and the shell had gone by special messenger to the ballistics department.

Only a large irregular stain now showed where the body of Ronald Tompkins had lain. The assistant medical examiner, a dark little man with gold-rimmed spectacles, had pronounced Tompkins dead of a bullet wound in the back.

The gun had been held rather close, he said moodily, pointing to the powder burns on the clothing. Then he had supervised the removal of the remains to Bellevue morgue, where it was at that moment being posted. The flashbulbs of the newspaper photographers outside had gone off in a dazzling chain reaction when the sheeted stretcher was carried to the dead wagon.

O'Callahan's heavy fingers paused in mid-air. He withdrew his steely blue gaze from McGann, wiped it across the drapes and used it neatly to impale Frazier Farwell, who jumped. The radio man now was wearing fawn-colored slacks, a soft shirt and a plaid sport coat which accentuated the putty-like color of his skin.

"And all you know, Mr. Farwell, is that Solly Spanish asked you about the layout of this house and whether Mr. Tompkins had said when he would go south this winter?"

Farwell nodded unhappily. "I—I just thought I ought to tell Ronnie," he croaked. "He was always damned decent to me."

The inspector's voice was edged. "You're sure, Mr. Farwell, that you didn't let your imagination get the better of you—so that Tompkins might feel obligated and react accordingly?"

A dull flush crept up above the collar of the sports shirt. But if Farwell had considered a sharp answer, he seemingly thought better of it. He said, "No."

O'Callahan sighed thoughtfully; the cottony eyebrows drew together. "All right," he said. "Both of you can go. And let me give a word of warning."

He gave considerably more than a word. He began by ac-
knowledging the splendid record of Mr. McGann in the Washington service with which he was personally familiar. He touched
upon the straightforward account of affairs that they had given.
He mentioned that he would be truly grieved if through careless-
ness they exposed themselves to the murderer of Tompkins, and
thereby increased the work of the department.

In conclusion, he would like to see them at the inquest set
for the following day. Meanwhile, they were to discuss the case
with no one. And, oh yes—one more point. Any boarding of fast
trains, speedy ocean liners or transcontinental planes would be
viewed with the deepest suspicion and alarm. "I wouldn't want
to have to lock you up in the Tombs as material witnesses," he
said in a voice which indicated that he would like nothing better.
Then he rose. "I'll see you to the door."

His broad back preceded them down the hallway, now brightly lighted by a strong bulb dug up by a patrolman in the storage
room. The inspector opened the door and an equally broad back
in blue moved aside on the front stoop. Instantly, half a dozen
flashbulbs went off.

Several men and women, who had been sitting on the front
steps, jumped up and moved toward the door. Leading was an
elderly man in a derby and a dusty coat.

"How about it, Inspector?" he said testily. "I've got a deadline
in half an hour."

The inspector glared sourly at the ladies and gentlemen of the
press. "I'll have a statement in five minutes," he said.

One of the girls said "Nuts." A dark young man with sharp
features beneath a crumpled fedora shoved his face forward. "We
want a look around inside," he said. "Our photographers want
some inside shots. We haven't—"

McGann stepped back so that they would not see him. Farwell, too, remained in the shadows. "Five minutes," Inspector

O'Callahan promised. He moved back and closed the door. "You can't go out that way," he told McGann.

In the end, they went down the back fire-escape to the court-yard. McGann noticed how quickly and quietly the iron extension went up. They passed through the next-door service hall to the front. McGann looked closely but saw nothing. He and Farwell walked rapidly west toward the park, heads down, hats pulled low over their eyes.

At Fifth Avenue, they stopped. Farwell seemed to have developed a slight tremor that moved in waves from his head to his toes. He said, "For a drink I'd pawn my typewriter on Yom Kippur—if it was Yom Kippur and I had a typewriter."

"I don't blame you," McGann said. "That was bad enough without a hangover."

"Going south?" the radio man asked. "I've just got time to get to my hotel and confer with my bartender. I'm on a midnight show and the way I feel now no record would be safe with me."

He held out a quivering hand which McGann found alarmingly cold. The detective shook it and said reassuringly, "You'll be all right. If you find time, play a little early Lombardo for me."

Farwell grinned weakly. But the request seemed to buck him up. "Glad to," he said. He waved wildly at a southbound cab which stopped suddenly.

"Go ahead," McGann said. "I'm walking a bit."

Farwell darted across the street, and the cab door slammed behind him. The cab had hardly pulled away before the detective noticed a dark car without markings swing around the corner, and glide after it. Two men sat stolidly in the front seat, their eyes on the cab ahead.

The detective smiled grimly. There was nothing, he thought, like the trust of a forthright character such as Deputy Inspector C. P. O'Callahan. 'Twas a thing to warm the hardest heart, and sure 'twould make you worship the ground they'd throw in his face someday.

He wondered how many men were tailing him. Probably two, at least. They'd sit in the car unless he ducked into a subway and then one would have to hit the pavement. The other would hang around a while, then go back to headquarters and wait for contact to be reestablished.

McGann walked south. The night air was clean and cool. From the corner of his eye, he saw another car pull around into Fifth and slide to the curb across the street. Shadow the shadow, he thought.

He glanced at his wrist-watch as he passed under a street light. It was 9:50. The Fifty-Ninth Street plaza was just three blocks away and he had ten minutes. The way Chary Jones had looked at him, he could have fifty years.

Still, she might show up. And certainly he wanted to talk to her alone. Before O'Callahan or any of his lieutenants got there. She might know something important without even realizing it. Had Tompkins really loved her? Had he confided anything to her? Had she loved him?

Mrs. McGann's little boy was going to look like a great detective in the daily prints, he thought with a shudder. His fine new agency was due for a million dollars worth of publicity—all bad. Still, he had a choice: he could either solve the case or apply for a bakery route in East Orange.

Yes, it was going to be a great advertisement. Call on the McGann protective agency but first make your will. He'd like to see Ronnie Tompkins' will. Now there would be a juicy item for all concerned . . .

Slowly, the trailing car eased to the curb, behind him and across the street. McGann stepped briskly over 60th Street, seemed about to pass in front of the Sherry-Netherland. Suddenly he turned left instead and ran lightly down the steps of the BMT subway. He pressed a coin into the slot and clicked through the turnstile, then moved swiftly to the edge of the platform and put a post between himself and the steps.

In a moment there was a fearful clatter on the stairs and a bulky figure shoved through the turnstile. McGann peeked around his post. The figure moved agitatedly along the platform and a red face swung jerkily to and fro.

McGann came around, pushed a penny into the peanut machine and began a spirited struggle with the mechanism. The bulky figure subsided at sight of him and the red face was poked innocently into a tabloid the headlines of which screamed, "Ronnie Tompkins Murdered!"

McGann sauntered to the far end of the platform. He noticed that Red Face was content to sidle to the middle of the station where he could still keep his quarry in view. A faint roar far down the track mounted steadily in intensity. With a final shattering blast the train raced into the station, halted with a violent lurch. Automatic doors slid back and a score of passengers stepped off.

McGann got on. So did Red Face and a dozen others. McGann stayed close to his door. For a moment the train hesitated at the now empty platform. Just as the door started to close, McGann hopped back to the platform.

The train started, gathering speed quickly. McGann thought he could see Red Face glaring through a window of the departing car. He looked around swiftly. The place was almost deserted.

Ahead of him stretched an almost interminable platform leading away from the kiosk where he recently had descended. That entrance now would be strictly off limits. Red Face's partner undoubtedly was sitting up there in his car watching, just in case he slipped away and tried to backtrack. The maneuver he had in mind should bring him out somewhere else—at a point where he could not reasonably be expected.

He walked as fast as he could without attracting undue attention until the platform ended in a flight of stairs leading upward and he had to emerge. When he finally gained the sidewalk he had to look around to orient himself.

Mole-like, he had passed under Fifth Avenue diagonally, under Fifty-Ninth Street, and was now on Central Park South, a good two blocks away from the point at which he had gone underground. He breathed a brief prayer of thanks for New York. Wonderful city—no matter how many times you went down into the subway, you never came up in the same place twice. Antidote for monotony, too.

He looked at his watch; it was 9:58. The stratagem which had sent Red Face on a ride would not necessarily give McGann the night in which to loiter. If he didn't succumb to apoplexy, too much to hope for, the tail would hop off at the next station, call headquarters and flash word by radio to his partner still in the car to be on special lookout.

However, he was not likely to do that. McGann grinned happily to himself. It would be too public an announcement that he had been ditched. No, the shadow probably would take the time to return on the next train, meanwhile preparing his story of how he had paused but a moment to assist the elderly lady only to find that his ungallant tailee had vanished.

Approaching the Plaza, he glanced across at Saint-Gaudens' bronze victory statue of William Tecumseh Sherman, and the line of horses and glistening carriages drawn up along the opposite curb.

Lamps flickered at the sides of the ancient vehicles. Some of the equally ancient drivers dozed on the high seats or stood beside the horses' heads. The hackies all wore tall silk hats and looked strangely incongruous against the backdrop of modern Manhattan.

The detective darted between moving cars and gained the Plaza proper. It was gratefully gloomy here; he could barely make out the graceful statue of the lady above the fountain. The waters had been turned off for the season, but there were still enough leaves on the trees to soften the glow of the avenue's lofty lights.

It was exactly 10 o'clock as McGann approached the fountain. Charity Jones was huddled forlornly on the stone ledge. She had the green coat drawn about her and the hatbox was on the flagstones. On top of it were the morning tabloids, the only newspapers out at that hour.

"I'm glad you waited," McGann said. She looked up and he could see the hurt shock on her face. Her voice was lower than he had remembered it from the house. "I didn't know what to do," she said. "I must have had ten cups of coffee in a little place over on Lexington, and a boy came in with the papers."

"I'm sorry," McGann said.

"Yes." She stood up, and he was surprised to see that for a model she was not tall. In heels she would barely come to his line of vision. "He was a dreadfully unhappy man," she said. "But to die like that—it—have they caught her?"

"Her who?" McGann said.

"Oh." One of the white gloves went to her lips as though a secret had escaped. She shook her head. "Really, I don't know why I said that. It's just . . . I guess"—she gestured helplessly—"well, there were so many women in Ronnie's life I just assumed—"

McGann nodded. "It's a natural assumption," he said. "Still I don't know why any of them should want to kill him. He always treated them generously, didn't he?"

He was looking around even as he spoke. The headlights of a car, which moved too slowly to please him, glided south along Fifth Avenue. McGann half swung, watching it from the tail of his eye. By this time, his chum could have returned from his impromptu journey.

Chary Jones bent and picked up the ribbon of the hatbox. She let the newspapers slide to the ledge. He could see her better when she again faced him. Her eyes were clear beneath level brows. "Mr. McGann," she said, "I realize now from the newspapers that you knew Ronnie was dead when I first came there tonight. You tried to break the news gently—"

"Well, there was more to it. I—"

"Please," she said. "That's all right. I appreciate it. I was terribly upset and confused so I waited in the restaurant and here partly to collect my thoughts and partly because you asked me to. But now I guess I'd better go."

"Where?" The car had swung right around the corner into 58th and was creeping west. If it was Snow White and Red Face they could not have seen him yet; when they spotted him they would either stop dead or speed around the block to find a better place at which to pull over and observe them.

"Why, home," she said. She paused, as if struck by a sudden thought. Her voice trembled faintly as she added. "Or perhaps I'd save everyone time and trouble if I went directly to the police and told them everything—just how I called there tonight and you—"

"No, don't do that," McGann said hastily. "It would only confuse them more." She had slipped her arms into the sleeves of the green coat now and he took her right arm just above the elbow. The car had swung right again, into the little street before the Plaza Hotel, and its course now would bring it closer to them every instant.

McGann thought rapidly. If Chary Jones had anything to hide, she was being amazingly cool about it. Was she even baiting him a little? She certainly was not the picture of the grief-stricken fiancée, whose dream of marital bliss had been punctured by a thirty-two.

"Move fast," he said. "Spies are closing in." He whirled her about and marched rapidly toward Fifty-Ninth Street and the waiting line of carriages on the far side. Her arm felt firm through the soft wool of the sleeve. When she appeared to hang back, he tightened his grip. "Just a few more minutes," he said urgently. "Highly important." She walked faster then and they dodged through traffic.

He helped her quickly up into a rubber-tired victoria and sprang after her. He thought, if they look for me in one of these things they've got more imagination than I give them credit for. He pulled the heavy blanket up until only his eyes could be seen above it.

The hack driver turned around, and looked in surprise at the blanket surmounted by a pair of eyes which seemed to have taken possession of the back seat. McGann's voice was muffled. "Through the park, James," he said. He saw the homicide car make a slow turn fifteen yards away, and he poked a warning finger out from beneath the blanket.

"Drive like the wind," he added dramatically, "or I shan't be responsible for the consequences!"

5

UP IN CENTRAL PARK

Stars swung low over the park, darting among the thinning branches of the trees. The driver, of course, had paid no attention whatever to McGann's exhortation. He had merely said, "Yes, sir!" and turned into the park at his usual deliberate pace.

The horse's hooves rang cleanly on the sharp air, the sound blending with the creak of leather and the low whir of the muted wheels. McGann had emerged from beneath the blanket which now covered their knees cozily. He looked at the girl whose head was bent slightly as she appeared to study her gloved hands. Lightly, the night breeze brought a breath of perfume from the shining tresses.

"Holmes would have sacked me for this," McGann said. "He never took the first carriage or the second, remember? That's probably Moriarty up there right now."

He stared belligerently at the wrinkled neck and high silk hat of the driver. A lamp-post glided by and in the yellow rays he could see that she was smiling.

"Mr. McGann," she said, "I'm not going to pretend to be heart-broken over Ronnie's death. I'm just terribly, terribly sorry for him, and I hope he's happier than he ever was here."

"Still you were going to marry him?" McGann said.

"I—I don't know." Her face was only inches from his, the eyes twin circles of darkness. "He thought I was. And I hadn't said no." She put her hand impulsively on his arm. "But, really, I hadn't said yes, either. I was going to ask him tonight for an—extension."

With many pauses, as the carriage followed the winding road north, Mary Margaret—otherwise Charity—Jones gave McGann a romantic fill-in. Like everyone else, she had read of Ronnie Tompkins' marriage marathon. Then, about six weeks before, when she had been modeling a chinchilla cape in a special show at the St. Regis, she had been approached by the manager.

"He was all excited," she recalled. "He said that Ronnie was there and had asked to meet me. The manager practically wept when I told him 'No, thanks.' So I gave in and Ronnie came up and said, 'How do you do will you marry me?'"

McGann got out his cigarettes. "Which question did you answer first?"

She sighed. "I said, 'How do you do why?' It seemed to surprise and fascinate him. I guess it never had occurred to him that a girl might hesitate."

"What else?"

Ronnie Tompkins had pressed the suit with exceptional ardor, she went on. He had said every extravagant thing except "I love you." He had showered her with fantastically expensive gifts, all of which she had sent back.

"You must have shattered his lack of faith in women," McGann said. He offered her a cigarette which she took, and he lit both.

"He certainly wouldn't take 'maybe' for an answer," she said. McGann asked bluntly,

"Why didn't you say no?"

She drew a quick breath. "Well, there were two reasons," she said almost defiantly. "The first is that I was really sorry for him.

Beneath that lady-killer surface, he was just a miserable little boy. He must have been almost desperate in his search for happiness, or he wouldn't have treated women the way that he did. I thought I might help him—call it a misdirected maternal urge if you want to."

McGann studied the star-blanketed heavens. He said gently, "The second was money."

Her dark lashes were half-moon brushes on her cheeks. "The second was money," she said. He had half-expected her to be angry, but if she was, she gave no sign. "Why should I deny it?" she said. "Modeling work doesn't last forever. And the few things I did on the radio didn't teach Mr. Hooper any new numbers."

"Dramatic?"

She gave a brief gesture of distaste. "Big parts on little stations. The renunciation scene from 'The Great Ziegfeld', a ten-minute version of 'The Cherry Orchard'—things like that."

"I should think your voice would be good."

She laughed aloud for the first time. He liked the mellow flight of sound. "Thank you," she said. "The trouble with my voice is that it says 'no' when third assistant producers want to drop up and go over the script."

They had reached 72nd Street and the carriage turned west to circle the lower park. Shining, low-slung cars purred past them, the walks and benches were almost deserted. The broad, imperturbable back of the driver was like a bulwark in front of and above them. McGann inhaled deeply, flicked the cigarette to the road. He asked, "Just why did you come to the Tompkins house at 6:50 o'clock tonight?"

Her momentary gaiety had vanished. "I was in the neighborhood on a job," she said. "Ronnie practically had made me promise to elope with him tomorrow night. I decided I simply had to have more time to think and I wanted to ask for it face to face—not by note or telephone . . ."

"And you just *happened* to be in the neighborhood on a job?"

"Yes."

"Can you prove that?"

She sounded surprised. "Do I have to?"

"Not to me," McGann assured her quickly. "I'm just a private detective. Legally, I can't even direct traffic. But the police might be skeptical. Maybe you'd better not say anything about it at all."

"If you think so," she said uncertainly. "Shall I go to them now?"

"I wouldn't," he said. "If they get any ambitious ideas, lawyers are hard to find at this hour and arranging bond is inconvenient." He was watching her sharply. "See them in the morning. Meanwhile, can you stay anywhere tonight besides home?"

Her brows drew together worriedly. "I can stay with my aunt," she said. "She lives just a few blocks from us"—McGann wondered why she hesitated and then it came out—"over on Tenth Avenue. It isn't a very nice neighborhood."

"It's a marvelous neighborhood," McGann said. He called to the driver to stop, and tossed the blanket aside. "We'll get a taxi on Seventy-Second Street. Next to North Clark Street in Chicago, Tenth Avenue is my favorite thoroughfare."

Charity Jones took his hand, and leaped lightly to the pavement. McGann passed several bills to the driver, who said, "*Thank you, sir.*" Chary laughed. "Now you know I'm from Hell's Kitchen."

"Source of our loveliest dishes," McGann said.

6
WATERFRONT MERGER

McGann spotted the figure huddled in the doorway across the street just after they stepped to the curb on Tenth Avenue. It was too late to duck. He told Charity Jones goodnight and watched her enter the tenement. He waited until she raised and lowered a fourth-floor window shade as a signal that she had gotten upstairs all right. Then he walked away, still pretending that he had not noticed the watcher. The man slid after him.

He thought, I've got more people following me than the Pied Piper. Heading west in Forty-Fifth Street toward the Hudson River, he was able quickly to determine that this was no professional stalker. Nor was the slight figure likely to be that of a plainclothesman.

A mugger? Possibly. But in view of the hectic evening it was much more likely to be someone connected in some way with the murder of Ronnie Tompkins. The killer? A chill skipped along his spine. If it was, and McGann was due for a .32 in the back, the killer would have to have a new gun. He had left the other one near the window of the Tompkins study.

Whatever his game, the tail was more energetic than polished. Swift glances usually caught him merging into the shadows of the next doorway.

McGann hurried toward the waterfront docks. Ahead of him stretched the ponderous elevated steelwork of the West Side express highway. Beyond it loomed the graceful shadows of giant ships. Not even the pollution along the docks could spoil completely the fresh, wet breeze of the great river.

Far out, a tug hooted and a ferry loosed a deep-voiced answer. Here were the black hulks of warehouses, the rough streets of heavy daytime commerce laced with shining railway tracks. Abruptly, McGann turned a corner. Off to his left, like a tremendous stage setting, glowed the city.

The detective took only a few steps from the corner, then slipped quickly into a dark and broken doorway. Footsteps slithered up. They rounded the corner. A shadow passed McGann and the detective moved lithely forward and whipped his left arm about the man's throat.

He jerked back, choking off the smothered cry, and slammed his left knee into the small of the man's back. The man was wiry but agile. He threshed wildly, and they danced across the sidewalk in deadly embrace. It took all of McGann's strength to hold the struggling trailer. He sucked in his breath with agonized effort. With ever-increasing pressure, he made sure that his opponent didn't breathe at all.

Gradually, the struggles lessened. McGann cautiously allowed his man a breath. When it did not set off any further atomic reaction, he gave him another. Still holding his left arm crooked about the man's throat, he frisked him expertly with his right.

There was no weapon so he released his hold. It felt good to let the blood run back into his aching arm. The man sat down on the curb and started to cough. He coughed and sobbed for air with his head down between his knees.

Then he sneezed twice. His hat had fallen off and he leaned over for it and he slapped it against his leg.

"Ya goddam fool," he said. "I think you fractured my esophagus."

McGann said, "Don't you know it's impolite to follow people?" He fished a cigarette from his pack, stuck it in his mouth and struck a match. After lighting the cigarette, he held the match in front of the man's face.

He had seen those sharp features before, and suddenly he thought of the stoop in front of the Tompkins home, and flashing bulbs. It was the dark young man in a crumpled fedora who had demanded admittance to the murder house for himself and news photographer.

"Hildy," McGann said, "don't ever sneak up on me again. You nearly went to that city room in the sky."

The reporter was tenderly pressing thin fingers against his neck. The match burned McGann's hand and he dropped it. He struck another. This time the glow revealed a pained grin. The reporter rose unsteadily, and clapped his hat back on. "Mr. McGann," he said, "my trailing days are over. From now on, I cover nothing but golden weddings and lodge meetings."

McGann was surprised. He said, "You name names?"

"I name *name*," the young man said.

They were in the dark again. Like a beacon far down in the cavernous tunnel under the highway shone the lights of a waterfront tavern. The detective tapped the other on the elbow. "Come," he said. "I would have words with you."

The bartender slid their third beers in front of Detective Mack McGann and Dinkman "Dink" Wexton, general assignments man of the *Morning Blade*. With a thick forefinger, he extracted a quarter from the change scattered on the moist mahogany in front of McGann. The barkeep's left ear was a sun-kissed cauliflower and his nose was a broken ski-slide.

He leaned forward between them. "Anything else, gents?"

"Yes," McGann said. "I'd like another one of those hard-boiled eggs. They're very good."

"Thank you, sir," the bartender said. He threw a light left jab at the bowl and lifted out an egg. He hooked it to the bar, crossing his right with the salt. He feinted another dime from the change, and stepped quickly to the cash register, balancing on the balls of his feet.

Wexton watched the performance with exaggerated interest. "What round is this?" he asked.

"Three," McGann said. "I think our man is winning on points."

The cash register bell rang and the bartender subsided, breathing deeply. He picked out a nickel change and slid it across to join the other coins in front of the detective.

Wexton looked at McGann and grinned crookedly. He had dark circles under his eyes which were, however, bright and alert. He winked and turned back to the bartender.

"Use your right a little more," he advised. "You could've nailed him twice that round."

The man behind the bar slid his head smoothly to the right, weaved back and to the left. He feinted briefly with his shoulder and clinched with the inner edge of the bar. "Naw," he said "I'm carrying him six rounds for the video rights."

Wexton stared. "I'll be damned," he said.

They had been there twenty minutes. A clock with a cracked glass above the bar said 10:55. Without appearing to, McGann had studied the newspaperman and he had not been displeased with the results. Dink Wexton was quick and sensible. Also, he probably knew more than anyone else about the late Ronnie Tompkins.

The reporter had explained everything with commendable lucidity. Some years before, he had covered the first of Ronnie

Tompkins' minute marriages. As such things will, it had started a trend in the city room of *The Blade*. From then on he had been required to cover all of them.

When the newspapers still were interested in interviews with Tompkins, Wexton automatically had drawn the assignment. He was the "Tompkins expert." If the art editor was too lazy to check the morgue and just yelled, "Hey, that Harmon dame. Wasn't she Tompkins' third wife?" Wexton called back, "No. She was the second."

He didn't even have to look it up. It was a convenience to have him around, like a highly-specialized almanac.

"I'd been expecting to hear from Tompkins," Wexton said. "That's why I wasn't surprised by the phone call."

That call, he told McGann, apparently had come in to the switchboard of *The Blade* in the early afternoon, before he had come on. Tompkins merely had left word that he would like to see Wexton any time that he could drop up before seven.

"It was a good excuse to get out of the office," Wexton had confessed to the detective. "I rolled around there about five and rang the bell half a dozen times but didn't get an answer. So I found a tavern over on Madison Avenue and had a sandwich and a beer or two. I went back to the house once and then hit the tavern again. I was just getting settled when blooie every squad car in the city goes by."

The beer was making McGann feel pleasant and relaxed for the first time in hours. He had his topcoat open and he had pushed his hat to the back of his head. He said, "So you followed the squad cars around the corner and were right there to cover the story?"

Dink Wexton's shoulders jerked in a gesture of contempt. "I bat my brains out writing about the guy for five years," he said, "and I get scooped on his murder. The headquarters man had the first flash." He swished the beer around in the glass until what was left was foam, and his eyes smouldered. "It proves," he said, "that clean living and right thinking are not their own rewards. That bastard O'Callahan wouldn't even let us in until he was damn good and ready."

McGann drained his glass and set it smartly on the bar. "High-handed," he said. "Very high-handed. Turn the power of the press on him. Call up and have them tear out the back page or something."

"Right!" Wexton bounced his puny fist off the mahogany. "I'll dictate a headline like Regis Toomey is always doing. I'll have O'Callahan transferred to Brooklyn."

"Brooklyn's too good for him. Better make it Staten Island. Something along the shore for the winter."

For a moment, they warmed to the inviting proposition. O'Callahan would, of course, be put back into uniform. The head on a one-column cut could read, "Back in Blue." All peddlers on his beat would sell nothing but waxed fruit; saloons would be constructed without side doors. Horse-room graft must be payable in Hungarian pengoes.

"No nursemaid would be less than ninety-five years old," Wexton enthused. "That'd kill the old sourpuss. He thinks he's distinguished with that white hair. Any dame that'd go for him would wait up for Santa Claus."

His interest abruptly diminished. "We overlooked one thing. *The Blade*."

McGann frowned. "You mean one word from you and they wouldn't stop the presses?"

Wexton shook his head slowly. "They wouldn't stop 'em if my tie got caught in the works."

They paused in contemplation of this horrendous mischance, and discovered that their glasses were empty. McGann gestured to the bartender, who bounced from his corner like Dempsey coming out for the eighth round in Chicago. "Once again, Mike," he said. The bartender nailed the empties neatly and weaved to the taps.

Reluctantly, McGann pulled his mind back to Wexton's recital of his earlier moves. He made several mental notes. "Look," he said. "You rang the bell at Tompkins' place at five o'clock the first time. You didn't get an answer. You went over to Madison Avenue but later tried once more. What time was the second try?"

Wexton scowled in thought. "Just before six. I couldn't figure it out. Ronnie was a screwball and all that but he didn't go around making phone calls for you to come up and then not let you in."

The reporter hesitated, as though weighing the advisability of further disclosures, then looked vaguely past the detective. "I walked around in back," he said.

McGann was instantly interested. "You did?" he said. "Was the light on in the study?"

"No," Wexton said promptly. "There wasn't a light in the place that I could see. I figured Tompkins had been called out suddenly, and either forgot about me or just couldn't get in touch."

"How about the fire escape?"

"What about it?"

"Was the extension to the ground up or down?"

Wexton looked surprised. "Hell," he said. "I guess it was up or I would have noticed it. I didn't pay any real attention."

McGann pondered. He had arrived at the Tompkins' home just a few minutes after six, and had been instantly admitted. Why had Wexton's ring been ignored and his own answered? It seemed hardly likely that Tompkins had been out and come home in those few minutes between callers. Anyway, hadn't Frazier Farwell been sleeping it off all of that time in an upstairs bedroom? Had Tompkins for reasons of his own decided not to admit the reporter until after he had talked with McGann?

The detective took another look at Wexton as the reporter lifted the glass of beer. His nose was rather long, the chin small but pugnacious. That hat had served two terms, and the topcoat was the kind where you walk up another flight and they give it to you. No, Wexton was not on any gravy train—or if he was, he was spilling as much as he was spending.

Yet many parts of his story did not jibe with the facts as Mc-Gann knew them. Why? He took a mouthful of the beer which was cool and sharp.

"How'd you happen to be watching the tenement on Tenth Avenue?" McGann asked.

Wexton crushed out a cigarette carefully, tracking down and extinguishing stray sparks with great deliberation. When he looked up his eyes gleamed above the brownish shadows. He said, "We're both in trouble, Mac. I missed a story and you loused up a case. Suppose we split our information? I can help you . . . you can help me."

"All right."

Wexton's voice dropped a notch lower. "I told you that I knew almost everything Tompkins did. If Ronnie didn't tell me somebody else always would. I knew about the Jones dame almost from the beginning."

McGann thought briefly of a serenely beautiful face, remembered the breath of perfume in the park. He said, "You thought she could tell you something about Tompkins' murder?"

Wexton shrugged. "It would at least be an interview with the only good-looking girl Ronnie didn't marry. A switch."

"And when you didn't find her at home you thought you'd check up on her aunt's place? I hope Brother O'Callahan isn't as sharp as that."

"You're on safe ground."

McGann changed the subject. "Has *The Blade* morgue got a good file on Tompkins?"

"Good enough. They stop picking horses every other day to clip the papers."

The detective glanced at the clock. "Let's put in a couple of hours reading up on our late friend. I need a fill-in."

"Okay," Wexton said. He slid from the stool. "But it will take longer than that. Remember it's been collecting ever since he proposed to his nurse."

7

THE BLONDE AT THE WINDOW

In McGann's dream, someone was rapping on a glass-topped desk. He could see the desk floating in front of him and make out the closed hand moving slowly up and down. The hand barely left the glass but the rapping was sharp and brisk.

It woke him up. He looked at the clock on the dresser. It said a quarter after nine so he had been asleep about five hours; he and Dink Wexton had spent most of the night going through the newspaper clippings and photos on the late Ronald Tompkins and his wives.

He shuddered at the thought of a mountain of pale yellow envelopes, each bulging with clippings. Some were new; others were brown and cracked with age. When they finished, McGann had been dusty but full of Tompkins knowledge. His eyes still smarted.

The crack of knuckles on glass resumed. He turned toward the fire-escape windows of the apartment bedroom and saw what had intruded upon his dream. It was a blonde. Her smooth yellow hair was pulled tightly toward the back of her head and she was holding one hand cupped at the left side of her face to shut out the light. She half crouched on the fire-escape, face up close to the glass and peering in.

McGann leaned on one elbow and studied her interestedly. She couldn't get in because the window that opened directly onto the fire-escape was locked, and the open one next to it was too far away to reach.

Her fingers fluttered in a tentative wave when she saw that he was awake. McGann waved back. She frowned impatiently and raised both hands, palms up. Her lips moved soundlessly to form the unmistakable command, "Let me in!"

McGann was sleeping raw. He replied with a circular motion of the hand meaning, "Turn around" and covered his eyes. She turned around. He got up, put on shorts and a robe and slippers. Then he walked over, threw off the window catch and raised the sash. He said, "Won't you climb in?"

A black suede pump was followed by a slim, bare leg, and the process was immediately repeated. McGann put a helping hand under the small of her back as she slid into the room.

"Thanks," she said, and straightened up. As soon as she looked at McGann she pursed her thin lips. "I thought you were dead, too," she said. "What the hell was the matter—overdose of Ovaltine?"

McGann rubbed his unshaven chin. "You wrong me," he said. "A detective to the core, I never sleep. I was feigning, Mrs. Tompkins. It is Mrs. Tompkins, isn't it—nee Irma Nelson?"

Wife No. 4 nodded her smooth blonde head, and brushed at her skirt. "Right with Eversharp," she said. She gestured toward the window. "I wanted to talk to you and I didn't think it was any business of that dizzy-looking detective in the lobby."

"So by coming up the fire-escape you think you are keeping him in total darkness?" Irma Nelson stared stonily. McGann clucked. "Wrong," he said. "The finest watch both front and rear. They know you're here, all right. I won't ask how you found my window."

At his gesture, she preceded him to the adjoining living room. "Good. I wouldn't want to tell on that wholesome-type janitor. Bet he gives you plenty of heat in the wintertime."

"He's a definite Vulcan," McGann said. He opened the door of the tiny kitchenette. "Coffee?" By the time the percolator was on, Irma Nelson Tompkins was reclining in McGann's favorite chair with bare knees crossed. She took a cigarette from the box on the coffee-table.

McGann took one, too, and held a light. She laid her cool hand over his to steady the flame, then looked up through lashes curiously dark against her sleek hair. For a moment he returned her gaze, then he decided that he'd better see if the coffee was doing anything yet. It wasn't.

"Stop jittering around," she said, "and tell me something. Who killed Ronnie? You?"

"Absolutely not," McGann said. "Word of honor. Did you?"

She gave him a slow smile that was without warmth. "Don't get me wrong, Handsome. If you had I wouldn't think any less of you and that's not because it's impossible. I knew Ronnie Tompkins backwards and he was asking for it."

McGann surveyed her speculatively. She was wearing a hint of greenish eye shadow, odd both for the hour and her coloring. Her pale left hand drooped languidly over the arm of the chair. She seemed completely without nerves.

"Don't talk like that in front of O'Callahan," he said. "He'll have you trying on chairs for size."

She dismissed the inspector with a flick of tapering fingers.

"Little Irma can take care of herself. What I wanted to ask you about was that pillow."

"The little one with the lace under Ronnie's head? What about it?"

"Well, did the police say anything about it while you were there? Anything that wasn't in the papers?"

"Wait a minute," McGann said. "Let's get this straight. You read about the pillow in the morning papers. You also read about me, complete with address, and clambered up here like Tarzan's mate. Why?"

"It's my pillow."

"Ah." The percolator started bubbling through the silence. Her gaze was locked with his, level and unblinking. He said, "I see. Your pillow. Odd little thing. A memento of what they call happier days? Something out of the long ago?"

"I left it there yesterday."

She was still featuring the candid "I-have-nothing-to-hide" look. McGann walked over and waited a minute before turning off the gas under the coffee. Tompkins might have gone to that nightclub beyond the horizon but he certainly had left a legacy rich in wackiness.

"You left it there yesterday?"

"Yes."

"Under his head?"

"Can the gaiety," Irma Nelson said. "I must have left it somewhere in that stuffy study of his. It was a dumb thing to do. My name's embroidered on it."

"That's a clue right up O'Callahan's alley," McGann said. "He learned to read at an early age and has never entirely forgotten. Suppose I pour this devil's brew and you tell me all about it?"

"Pour away."

Over the coffee-cups, Irma Nelson Tompkins explained. It was simplicity itself. She had remained friendly with her transitory husband; Tompkins had endeavored to maintain amicable relations with all of his ex-wives.

"I just dropped in to see Ronnie about one o'clock," she said. "It was something personal—that doesn't matter. I had that damn little pillow with me because I was going to stop in Altman's and try and get a box it would fit in."

"Where'd it come from?"

Oh, that. Well, Irma Tompkins had a six-year-old niece. Horrible brat but still she had her moments like when Irma had given her a doll and the kid had named it Irma. Kind of touching. So she had planned on giving the child a pillow for the doll carriage.

"That's why I embroidered the name on it," she explained. "You should have seen Solly's eyes when he found I could do it."

"Solly?" McGann's mind flashed back to the stacks of clippings of the night before. A Sobol column that said Irma "Blondeshell" Tompkins was showing a preference for Spanish omelets. Dorothy Kilgallen's item which wondered what midtown character had come down with Irmatitis. . . . He thought it best to let her make her own revelations. He said again, "Solly?"

"Solly Spanish, my dream boat. The only man of his kind in New York."

"Sounds lonesome. But go on. You saw Tompkins and then left, forgetting your niece's gift?"

"That's right. Like I say, it was a dumb thing to do. Talk about putting yourself on a spot. But who'd of thought anybody was going to plunk Ronnie?"

"Who indeed?" McGann said. He thought of the heavy draperies of the ex-wives' art gallery, the labyrinthean mazes of the old brownstone. He said casually, "So Ronnie saw you to the door and that was that?"

Her expression did not change but her eyes flickered and there was an expectant pause. She shoved the coffee cup back from the edge of the table. "I found my own way out," she said. The thin lips twisted bitterly. "I did it once before, you know."

"On April 11, three years ago," McGann said. "I've been cramming." He poured two more cups of coffee. "Not that I don't appreciate company at breakfast but why come to me?"

"I thought maybe you'd tell me what to do. Solly's really no help in a thing like this and would probably blow his top if he knew I had gone to see Ronnie."

"Go to the police."

"I don't like that either."

"You'll have to. Simply tell them what you've told me. They'll take a statement but you shouldn't have any trouble. Only you won't get your pillow back for a long time, if ever. It's evidence."

"Let the damn doll sleep in a chair." She relaxed with the smile of a person relieved to have found a course of action. "You're right, I guess. I'll try it."

McGann thought she'd leave immediately but she appeared still to be turning something over in her mind. At last she said diffidently, "Just in case you're interested, that Rogers dame could have had a grandstand seat for the fireworks."

"How's that?"

"She just got an apartment on the next street so her bedroom window is only across the court. I know Ronnie was mad as hell about it. Said in a town as big as New York why did she have to park so close."

McGann suggested sentimental reasons, an attachment for the neighborhood where Kathleen Rogers had spent the happy minutes of her married life. "Let's see," he mused, "weren't you her immediate predecessor?"

"I wouldn't be her anything."

"I mean Tompkins married her after—after you and he split?"

She rose. "Rogers was the consolation prize that year, yes. Anyway, I thought you might like to know about her place. Isn't that a clue or something?"

"It opens a fascinating vista," McGann said. He trailed her to the door. "Incidentally, how'd you like the Gobelin yesterday?"

"The which?"

"The tapestry. It must have been Tompkins' last acquisition, excepting the thirty-two in the back. He was raving how terrific it looked in the study."

"Oh, that." Her hand hovered above the knob. "Why, marvelous, I suppose, if you go in for that sort of stuff. But I liked it all right."

McGann nodded. "I thought you might."

She turned the knob without opening the door, then reached over and rubbed her left palm gently along his stubbly cheek. Her eyes crinkled. "Come out from behind that hedge some day and let me see you," she said. "I may like the result."

McGann patted her shoulder. "From this day forward my window is always open. Climb up any time."

She went out, closing the door gently.

8

DIAGRAM OF DEATH

McGann was working shaving soap into his beard when the buzzer sounded. He swung the door open, wondering what Irma Nelson had forgotten, and Dink Wexton walked in.

The reporter leered pleasantly. "It must be wonderful to be a detective," he said. "You meet so many."

"I deduce that you saw Mrs. Tompkins—Irma?"

"In the flesh. Pink, that is."

"There's coffee on the stove," McGann said. He returned to the bathroom washbowl and was executing neat furrows with the safety razor when Wexton came in with a cup. He eased down on the seat lid. "All right, give."

McGann gave. "It's pretty obvious that she was lying all of the way through," he concluded.

"You mean the tapestry gag? I don't remember seeing any in the study last night but then I wasn't looking for it."

"There wasn't any. She took a chance and guessed wrong. I'm still wondering why she came up at all unless she wanted to give the Rogers woman some trouble."

Wexton shrugged. He drank the lukewarm coffee and seemed lost in thought. Then he balanced the cup on the edge of the washbowl and took a folded sheet of copy paper from his inside coat pocket. "I've got news for you," he said. "They've traced the gun."

"Wonderful. Who to?"

"Ronnie Tompkins."

"Ugh!" McGann splashed water over his face. "I was afraid of that. Details?"

Dink Wexton had them. The murder weapon had been a Colt .32 automatic purchased by Ronnie Tompkins two years before. He had kept it in the upper right-hand drawer of the desk in his study and had a permit for it. The permit had been properly re-newed and was good until December 31.

"One bullet had been fired and there were seven left in the clip," Wexton read from his notes.

"How about the bullet in the body? I presume Brother Tomp-kins surrendered it without further struggle?"

"He didn't say a word." Wexton checked off the additional information—hard metal-jacketed with six narrow rifle markings slanting right to left from base to dome. "The ballistics boys said it was fired from that gun, all right."

"And that ejected shell?"

Firing pin markings jibed, Wexton related, proving that the shell had come from the Tompkins gun. The mark left by the ejector mechanism was corroborative proof. He said, "One gun, one shell, one bullet, one corpse."

"No fingerprints, I suppose? Never got one off a gun yet."

"Nope. Clean as a beagle's bicuspid."

During the exchange, McGann had dressed. He tightened his tie and pushed a hat on his head. "I have been cordially invited to attend the inquest, or else," he said. "Ride along?"

"Absolutely. The desk says I'm to stick to you like yester-day's band-aid. One more miss and I'm back to second-string copy-boy."

"I'll tip you off with my dying breath."

In the lobby, McGann nodded pleasantly to a heavyset man whose plainclothes calling was not difficult to fathom. He could see why even Irma Nelson had been alerted and had chosen to detour. The plainclothesman returned the nod, followed them out and climbed into his car while they hailed a cab.

They were rolling downtown when Wexton pulled a copy of the morning *Blade* from his topcoat pocket and handed it over. "Read all about it," he said.

"Swell," McGann said. "Is Dick Tracy still trapped in that bubble bath?" He spread out the Page One banner, SEEK MYSTERY BLONDE IN TOMPKINS SLAYING. "What's this?"

"Second day lead."

"Hmm," McGann said. He scanned the story quickly. "A mysterious blonde was being sought throughout the city today by a score of detectives investigating the weird slaying of playboy Ronnie Tompkins. The much-married copper heir was found shot to death—"

"It doesn't say who she is," McGann complained.

Wexton grinned. "It never does. In this business you always have to look for a mysterious blonde the day after a murder. You can't write a story saying the victim is still dead."

"Don't you ever look for a mysterious man?"

Wexton looked shocked. "Do you want to put us out of business?"

McGann handed the newspaper back. "Bring me an extra the day you find her."

"Don't worry, we'll never do that. It would set journalism back fifty years." He turned to page two. "Here's something, though. They can't account for one cartridge."

Wexton proceeded to read a short item about the box of .32 calibre cartridges which O'Callahan's men had found in the drawer of Tompkins' desk. It was designed to hold fifty bullets but there were only 41 in the container when police discovered it.

"Forty-one in the box, seven in the gun and one in Comrade Tompkins," he added. "Grand total—forty-nine. Bullet, bullet, who's got the bullet?"

The cab spun past the soaring Empire State, began to squeal protestingly as the Fifth Avenue lights ahead flashed red. McGann studied the plaque on the cab partition which said that the vehicle was being driven by Joseph V. Romano No. 78620.

"That could be important," he said. "On the other hand, Tompkins might have fired a test bullet at the butler to see if the gun worked when he got it."

"I wouldn't have put it past him. Sometimes his humor was on the pixie side."

As the cab rolled through Union Square, Wexton read excerpts of quotes from several ex-wives. "Here's one from Faith Starr in Cannes," he said. "Ronnie wasn't killed by a trans-Atlantic rocket so she's in the clear. She says, and I quote, 'I will always have a soft spot in my heart for Ronnie. He was a true gentleman and one of the finest husbands I ever had.'"

"A touching tribute," McGann said. "Any more?"

"A wire from Gladys Mars in Hollywood. Tompkins took her out of a chorus. She was his first wife so she always felt that the other gals were loser's choice."

Gladys stated that the news saddened her, Wexton read, and she hinted that a suicide theory should not be too lightly dismissed. "Dear Ronnie," she said, "never quite recovered from the shattering of our idyll. I had long feared that he might do something desperate . . ."

Wexton threw the newspaper on the seat. "The most desperate thing Tompkins would do over a woman would be to drink a glass of domestic champagne." He pondered. "Of course that might have killed him."

McGann asked, "Did Tompkins drink very much?"

"Steadily, but he always had it under control. I never saw him really plastered but then again I never knew him to pass one up."

They were moving through Worth Street, approaching the new skyscraper housing the offices of the New York medical examiner and other municipal officials. "Across the street is all right, Joe," McGann told the driver. He paid the meter, added a tip. "Well, something caught up with him yesterday afternoon. He let me drink alone."

The reporter shook his head. "First time for everything. In Ronnie's case, first and last. But then you never could tell what he'd do next."

There were several newspaper photographers at the door of the building. Some had tripods set up, others swung speed graphics by the strap. One called, "Mind posing for a shot, Mr. McGann?"

"A pleasure," McGann said. He paused just below the top step and smiled. "How's this?"

"Perfect. Get the hell out of there, Wexton. This is for a family newspaper."

There was a busy clatter of plates, the click of shutters. "Just one more, Mr. McGann." There was a flurry of clicks. "How do you spell that, M-a-c?"

"Mc," McGann said. "You may describe me as the detective who unsolved the case." He pushed gently past. Wexton again gained his side in the towering lobby. There was a girl at the information desk. McGann asked, "The Tompkins inquest, please?"

"Second floor auditorium."

"Thank you." They went up. There were a couple of dozen persons in the huge place. O'Callahan was up at the bench with the men from the medical examiner's office. He acknowledged McGann's greeting.

"It's a good thing you got home when you did this morning," he said jovially. "We were going to notify the police."

McGann matched his seeming good humor. "That would have been embarrassing, Inspector. I told my friend I was sitting up with a sick wife."

"We've got a couple of new questions."

"Any time, Inspector. If you're not ready to start yet could I see the autopsy report?"

O'Callahan gestured toward the dark little man with gold-rimmed spectacles whom McGann remembered at the Tompkins' home. "Go ahead. Dr. Scholz will take care of you."

Dr. Scholz gloomily produced an autopsy chart which showed front and back drawings of an extremely unprepossessing male character. Someone had typed in information as to Tompkins' approximate age, weight, height and other data at the top of the official paper.

A red dot had been placed high on the left back of the figure. McGann and Wexton flanked Scholz while the medico expounded as if lecturing a class in anatomy.

"The bullet entered the back through the intercostal muscles between the fourth and the fifth ribs and four inches to the left of the midline. It entered the pleural cavity, passing through the left lung and entering the pericardial sac posteriorly."

He warmed to his subject. "Passing through the right ventricle and the anterior aspect of the pleural cavity, the bullet came to rest against the posterior wall of the sternum "

"I get it," Wexton said. "Now just where is that in relation to Lindy's?"

Dr. Scholz's spectacles glittered. "He was plugged right through the ticker. Death was practically instantaneous."

McGann made some notes. "Then the bullet followed a level course?"

"Yes."

"Fine. Thanks. One other thing. You say the bullet stopped at the sternum. It didn't break through at all?"

"No breakthrough."

Several other reporters saw Wexton aping McGann's notes and came over. They took down the same information and asked what importance it had if any. A girl from INS rubbed a pencil along her cheek, leaving a gray smudge. She said, "Can't you tell the height of the murderer or something from tracing the course of the bullet?"

McGann smiled. "Pretty much guesswork."

They pressed the point. "But Tompkins was about five feet, ten. If another person just about the same height raised a gun and shot wouldn't it hit right where it did?"

"Suppose it was a murderer nine feet tall who shot from the hip?"

The man from the *Mirror* hopped on that one. "Hey, that's great. Suspect Circus Giant in Tompkins Death. A natural. Didn't Tompkins have a piece of Ringling Brothers or something?"

"Wait a minute, wait a minute," McGann pleaded. "I was just showing the fallacy of that theory. It doesn't hold water. A bullet could follow that course if it was fired by a midget standing on a spinet piano."

"Even better," the Mirror reporter enthused. "Midgets are terrific stuff. Remember the time they put one on J. P. Morgan's lap? Gives the whole thing a sort of Lon Chaney atmosphere."

"Shut up, Charley," Wexton said. "You're off the beam."

The reporter subsided, but with a grumble. "What are you trying to do—throw the story down? Trouble with you guys . . ."

"Excuse me," McGann said. He had seen Frazier Farwell entering the room. The disc jockey stopped just inside the door and looked around, smiling in recognition as McGann approached.

"Greetings," Farwell said as they shook hands. "Is this where we respin the platter?"

"Without even changing the needle," McGann said. His companion of the evening before looked considerably better. "I don't think much will come of it, though."

Police had rounded up passersby as members of the jury, and they were now being herded into the box. Farwell nodded toward the front row of the auditorium where an elderly wisp of a man sat somewhat apart with a prim woman. The man frequently tugged at the collar about his thin neck.

"There's the Pearsons," Farwell said. "He was Ronnie's butler and doubled as chauffeur. She was the maid with help once in a while from a cleaning woman."

McGann looked at them with interest. "I understood they had yesterday off. Did you see them at all?"

Farwell passed a hand over his eyes. "God," he said, "I don't really remember. I just have flashes—babbling to Ronnie, falling into bed." He took a deep breath. "Never again . . . I hope . . . I hope . . . I hope. . . ."

With several sharp raps, the medical examiner called the session to order. As McGann and Farwell took seats, McGann felt someone's gaze upon him. He looked up and met the frosty blue eyes of Inspector O'Callahan. The joviality of only a short time before seemed already to have passed.

McGann sighed. "If Glocca Morra needs a sheriff," he said, "O'Callahan has a vote."

9

PERSONS UNKNOWN

The inquest moved swiftly. O'Callahan took the stand and told of leading the investigators to the Tompkins home. Farwell related his story, apparently embroidering a trifle the amount he remembered up to the time McGann pounded on the upstairs door.

"Step down," the medical examiner said. "Ambrose Pearson."

Pearson seemed stunned into an unnatural calmness. Yes, he had worked for Mr. Tompkins for fifteen years. His employer had been somewhat eccentric but not unkindly. For instance, he had been pleasant about allowing the couple to have the previous afternoon off.

"What time did you last see Mr. Tompkins alive?"

The butler shifted. That, he said, had been about noon when he told Mr. Tompkins that he and his wife would greatly appreciate the rest of the day to visit an ailing relative in Jamaica.

"He said it would be all right. I took the car around to the garage and left it for servicing. When I came back I went into our quarters downstairs, and waited for Mrs. Pearson to get ready."

"What time did you leave the house?"

That, Pearson said, was nearly one-thirty. As they emerged from the street-level doorway at the side of the brownstone steps they had seen Mr. Farwell on the outside landing above. They had hurried on their mission.

"To visit this sick person?"

To McGann's amazement, the butler slowly began to turn crimson. He tugged unhappily at the large collar. "I'm afraid, sir, that the reason given for our leaving was not the—ah, completely unvarnished truth." He gulped. "While we do have relatives in Jamaica, none was ill at the moment."

The medical examiner laid down his pencil and faced the witness with new interest. "Am I to understand that you told your employer a deliberate falsehood in order to obtain the afternoon off?"

Pearson was blazing now. "Yes, sir."

"You realize that you are under oath here?" The question thundered in the silent room. "Where did you really go?"

"On a bird walk."

"A what?"

"A bird walk. You walk through the woods and look for birds. Yesterday it was Croton-on-Hudson. Many people do it, sir"— the butler's voice was urgent—"it's healthful and educational."

The medical officer looked disappointed. "Then you saw nothing?"

"On the contrary, sir." Pearson seemed to have found fresh confidence in the recollection of carefree hours in the wilds of Croton-on-Hudson. He beamed. "We saw a yellow-bellied fly-catcher!"

There were assorted snorts from the press row. The official banged his gavel and his brow gathered storm clouds. "I mean anything pertinent to this inquiry?"

"Oh, no, sir."

"Then step down. Mr. McGann."

McGann identified himself and touched briefly on his service with the FBI. He described the summons to the Tompkins home, and told of being upstairs with Farwell when the shot rang through the house.

The press row scribbled busily when McGann pulled out his notebook and recounted the various incidents related by his eccentric host as possibly portending violence.

"Did you receive any cash retainer?"

"I did not."

The medical examiner allowed a note of sympathy to creep into his voice. "Then the sudden demise of your client deprived you of what looked like a lucrative case?"

"It did." From the corner of his eye, McGann had been observing Inspector O'Callahan write a note which an assistant passed up to the bench.

The official read it and hunched forward. "When you broke into the room and found the body of Mr. Tompkins you touched nothing?"

"Only the telephone, to call headquarters."

"You are certain of that?"

"Absolutely." What the hell, McGann thought, O'Callahan is looking pleased. Swiftly, he reviewed the moments in the study. No, he was sure that he had been meticulous in preserving evidence for the regular authorities.

The examiner cleared his throat. "Is there any other statement you would like to make in the case at this time, Mr. McGann?"

Instinctively, McGann sensed a trap. There was something else in the wind. He wondered if they had learned of that inopportune visit by Chary Jones; the call he had purposely neglected to mention.

If that were brought out now it might put him in a dubious light but it was hardly criminal. He decided to adopt a frank and candid air.

"Only that I will feel personally responsible until the murderer is found."

"Thank you. Step down, please. Dr. Scholz."

The assistant medical examiner told of pronouncing the victim dead, and of finding the bullet wound in the back. Again the chief officer consulted O'Callahan's note.

"When you prepared the body for autopsy did you notice anything else unusual?"

Scholz seemed prepared for this. "Yes. There was a postmortem lividity of the left chest—a widespread discoloration at that spot."

"And medically what did you infer from that?"

Scholz looked directly at McGann. "That the body had been moved. That is, that it had not always been on its back as I found it."

McGann breathed easier. If O'Callahan and his aides wanted to get bogged down in medical details, let them go to it. He knew what he had seen and done. Painful experience had taught him that if one doctor could be found to testify in a certain direction, six could be produced to refute him.

Scholz explained that a prone body would hemorrhage into the chest, leaving a mark that would remain even if the body later was turned on its back. After a few more technical details, including the course of the bullet, he was excused.

The jury was hurried through its routine paces which were climaxed when the foreman stumbled through reading of the verdict on a slip of paper shoved into his hand. "We find that the deceased, Ronald Tompkins, came to his death at the hands of a person or persons unknown."

As the gavel banged, the reporters rose and hurried past the telephones in the lobby to the corner saloon where they could take turns at the lone booth. Wexton looked longingly after them but stayed near McGann who was approached by the inspector.

"You understand now," O'Callahan said, "that very little gets by us, Mr. McGann. While we don't refuse information from any source, we don't like tampering."

McGann felt his anger rise. There was obviously no use in further appeasement. "Listen, you big squarehead," he said. "If you think I shot my best client to keep him from writing me a check, go ahead and arrest me. I want to see the D.A. when you tell him the motive."

The blue eyes were suddenly innocent. "Who said you shot anybody?"

"And take that tail off me." Already he felt annoyed with himself for letting O'Callahan get his goat. "If I want a cop I'll call one."

"All right, all right." The strong, blunt hands made calming gestures. "No need to get excited. But you can see my position; the Commissioner is getting impatient."

"Sorry," McGann said, "but he isn't any more impatient than I am. I have more reason than you for wanting to see this case solved. If I get onto anything worthwhile, I'll let you know." He turned on his heel and walked out.

Wexton wisely said nothing until they were speeding uptown in a cab. Then he ventured, "The inquest clears everything up. All we have to do is grab persons unknown and rubber-hose a confession out of 'em before home edition time."

McGann grunted and lit a cigarette. "Don't you have to call your office?"

"Not on the inquest. We had another man there for that. For better or for worse, I am attached to you."

McGann was going to say, "'Til death do us part' but thought better of it. Instead, he said, "I've got to drop into my own office for a while. You can do a job for me."

"Swell." Wexton rubbed his thin hands. "Just put me on the trail. I'm the original human rumhound, I mean bloodhound."

"All right. Here." McGann jotted down names of several nightclubs on the back of one of his cards. He spoke again of the short thickset man and the dark-haired girl who were suspected of having followed Tompkins on the previous Thursday night.

"Get hold of the waiters who usually drew the Tompkins table. See if they remember any couple like that in the place. You ought to be able to reach them at home. Find out what you can and check with me at the office."

"Right!" Wexton hopped out at Forty-Second Street, palpably pleased with his sleuthing assignment. McGann's driver swung right and several blocks farther east pulled to the curb at a skyscraper office building.

McGann's secretary seemed relieved when he entered. She nodded toward the small waiting room in warning, and crooked a finger. McGann leaned over the low railing.

"A lawyer named Holton," she said. "Amos Holton. It's something to do with the Tompkins estate. He's been here fifteen minutes."

McGann went in and shook hands with a thin, baldish man whose black mustache was too heavy for his fine features. Mr. Holton accepted a chair, refused a cigarette and exploded a bomb.

"My firm is executor of the estate of Ronald Tompkins," he said. "Though Mr. Tompkins had not confided to us any fears for his life, we have decided to retain your services in his . . . ah, posthumous behalf."

McGann nodded solemnly. He hoped that this was not some sort of oral mirage which would suddenly end and be replaced by "Howdy Doody."

"Poor Mr. Tompkins," the voice went on, "had his own ideas about many things but he was not entirely without foresight. Some thousands of dollars always were deposited with us for emergencies." Mr. Holton dug into his briefcase and produced a check. McGann saw his own name and the sum of $2,500.

He accepted it delicately. "Extremely thoughtful," he said.

Amos Holton brushed his mustache with a pencil-thin forefinger. "We have the utmost confidence in the constituted authorities. However, we feel that no stone should be left unturned in seeking the slayer of our—and now your—client. There is, of course, a proviso."

"Natch."

"I beg pardon?"

"A colloquialism meaning 'quite so.'"

"Hmm. Well, be that as it may, the firm of Holton, Bolton, Durstine and Schwab must insist that you keep us informed of your progress." McGann nodded and the lawyer added, "I believe that you will have an excellent opportunity to further your investigation tonight. Mr. Tompkins is giving a party."

Oh, oh, McGann thought, I have been had. This character undoubtedly has a whole briefcase full of rubber checks, and is enjoying a field day. He said with gentle sadness, "Mr. Tompkins is dead. Remember?"

The ghost of a smile lifted the over-shadowed lip. "I am well aware of that. Our client was also thoroughly resigned to the inevitability of his taking-off. He long ago made provision for it."

Swiftly, the attorney sketched the session of several years before when Ronnie Tompkins had given orders for the handling of his affairs in the event of his death. He had asked that his body be cremated privately, but that his ex-wives and select friends gather in gay farewell as soon as possible at the Tompkins mansion. No expense for their entertainment was to be spared.

McGann said, "Just a minute. Do you mean that Tompkins feared for his life that long ago?"

The other gestured. "No, not at all. This was to be done whenever and for whatever reason the end came. Mr. Tompkins really had some unique ideas. For instance, tonight he will read his will."

"He . . . will . . . read . . . his . . . will?"

"Exactly. He made a record. There is also a document to take care of the legal aspect but he seemed to take particular delight in preparing this transcription of his bequests in his own voice. I will play it for the assembled guests."

"This I must hear and see," McGann said. "Tonight, you say?"

At ten, Holton revealed. Since there were no blood relatives and the body already had been released by the medical examiner's office, the cremation would take place that afternoon. The press would be barred from the evening affair.

"It would facilitate matters if you could escort Miss Jones," Holton said, referring to his notes. "While she never became Mrs. Tompkins, our client especially ordered that equal importance be given whatever young lady happened to be what he called 'in the works' at the time of his death."

Again McGann nodded. "Does Miss Jones know of this assignment of mine?"

"Yes. I may say that she appeared pleased when it was explained."

"You've had a lot of acceptances—to the party?"

Holton closed his briefcase and stood up. "I have never known guests to be so eager." He hesitated. "I, myself, am meeting Miss Mars at the airport and will be her escort for the evening."

McGann followed him to the door. "One thing more," he said. "Black tie?"

Holton gazed at him solemnly. "Natch," he said.

10

WEEP NO MORE, MY LADIES

The farewell party for Ronnie Tompkins seemed already well under way when McGann handed Chary Jones through the door. Soft lights made the carpeted hall feel even warmer after the crisp night. From somewhere inside, a peal of shrill laughter overrode the drone of voices; an accordion and a guitar were doing "Manhattan Serenade" in an exaggeratedly fast tempo.

Chary Jones half turned as the wave of sound engulfed them. Her eyes, when they met McGann's, were filled with unspoken dread. "I really don't think I can do it," she said. "It's too—too ghoulish."

McGann was watching her closely. "It was his last wish," he reminded. "You can bet the others are all here." He sent the blade home. "If you don't stay, it might look suspicious."

She bit her lip, appeared to struggle for a fresh hold on herself. While she was wavering, McGann handed his hat and coat to the butler. He asked the man, "How are the birds?"

Pearson's face was a genteel mask. "The birds, sir?"

"At Croton-on-Hudson. Incidentally, why go so far? Get off at Ossining some time. You can study the black-striped jailbird in its native habitat."

The butler smiled faintly. "I'm afraid you're making a joke, sir."

"Thank you," McGann said. "And you're right to be afraid of them." He turned to the girl. "Decided?"

She was pale. "Yes, I'll go through with it." The butler murmured that the ladies' wraps were being left on the second floor and she started up the long staircase, gold slippers glinting against the dark rug.

Party noises swelled momentarily as a door was opened and closed. McGann saw Amos Holton, the attorney, approaching. In formal clothes he looked more than ever like an undertaker. Even his smile had an embalmed look. His thin hand snaked forward.

"Ah, good," Holton said. "If you have a minute, I'll show you where we'll hear the will."

He led the way back to the study. McGann noticed that the smashed door had been replaced with one of lighter wood. A cheerful fire again blazed in the room, and a throw-rug covered the place where he knew an irregular stain to be.

Folding chairs had been arranged in quarter circles at one side of the room. Directly in front of the late host's desk, an expensive radio-phonograph combination glistened. Holton looked satisfied. "Everything is just as he ordered it."

McGann stroked the satiny finish of the phonograph. "Quite a machine," he said. "Isn't this the model that plays twelve ten-inch records and dances with you if necessary?"

"Mr. Tompkins always had the best of everything," Holton said smugly.

McGann thought of the portraits in the art gallery. "I'll believe that," he said. He thought of something else. "Any police here tonight?"

"No. They told me that they had searched the house thoroughly, and it could now be put into our hands as executors. As for reporters"—he grimaced in distaste—"we have seen to it that they stay out."

"Splendid," McGann said. "A motley crew. Lower the tone of any gathering." He thought of Dink Wexton that afternoon when the newspaperman had reported back and heard about the farewell shindig from which members of the fourth estate would be barred.

Wexton had sneered openly. "That just shows how well they knew Tompkins," he had said. "If they crab his publicity he'll come back and haunt them." So far, the reporter had had no luck in tracing the mysterious couple noted on Tompkins' trail. He had left McGann with a cryptic, "I'll see you sooner than you think."

"I've asked Mr. Farwell to lend us his professional services tonight," Holton's voice cut in. His tone was apologetic. "Since he handles records constantly, I thought I would have him play the will—I'm all thumbs on such gadgets."

"Has Farwell heard the record yet?" McGann asked sharply.

"Oh, no, it's in the wall safe. I won't even take it out until we're ready."

"Then he doesn't know what he'll be playing?"

Holton's eyes were onyx-black in his pale face. "You and I, Mr. McGann, are the only ones aware of the voice we are to hear tonight."

McGann looked about the room where death had stalked and thought of the voice now locked in the vault—the voice that soon would address them from the grave. "I've really got to hand it to Ronnie," he said. "He got the jolliest ideas."

"A wonderful client," Amos Holton said sadly. "Arranging divorce settlements alone kept us quite busy."

They were walking toward the front of the house when McGann heard the soft shush of light feet on thick carpet and Chary Jones came down the stairs. She smiled with regained composure, the green-brown eyes bright with excitement, and laid a hand lightly on the arm McGann extended. He said, "Shall we join the ladies?"

"Let's. And the men, too."

The gay wake struck them full as they entered the art gallery where it was centered, apparently in conformity with Tompkins' instructions. Now blue smoke stood in layers across the luxurious room. The seven lovely paintings glowed softly down from the walls and new light brackets lent aid to their struggle against the smoky haze.

Their entrance failed to interrupt an animated babble that rose from a score of men and women who stood or sat drinking in the room. Over in the corner a bar had been set up and the white-jacketed bartender was vigorously shaking a cocktail. The clinking of the ice was an off-beat to the music of the strolling troubadours who were working on "You Can't Marry Ten Pretty Girls."

"An oldie," McGann said. "I'll bet Tompkins ordered it." He hummed along with the guitar and accordion. "He died trying," he said. Her hand tightened on his arm.

"I'd like a cigarette, please."

He held a light. Her full lips closed over the cigarette, left a bright red smear as they came away. A lot of the guests were admiring the various portraits and McGann turned Chary toward her own. They looked at the serene face with its faint smile. "Lovely girl," McGann said. "We should meet and start making beautiful Muzak together."

Her shoulders shook a little. "Perhaps it can be arranged. I'd suggest you take her for a ride in the park."

"Not unless I get to drive the horse." He looked around. A waiter in a short white jacket was serving drinks from a large tray, slowly moving their way. He held the tray out and men and women were placing their empty glasses on it, taking fresh ones with hardly a pause in their conversation.

McGann watched them apprehensively. "We're too far from the base of supplies," he said. "Those desert rats will clean him out."

The waiter glanced up and suddenly began heading straight for them, threading his way through a group which sent annoyed looks at his back. He proffered the tray with a flourish. McGann was surveying it with interest when he heard a familiar voice.

"You're a detective," the voice said. "See if you can find the onion in one of these martinis." McGann glanced up into Dink Wexton's lopsided grin.

"That's too tough," McGann protested. "You got to start me out on the easy ones." He selected drinks for the girl and himself, then grinned back at the reporter. "I trust your card is paid up in the waiters' union?"

"Local 802," Wexton said. "Better get these fast. We may strike any minute for more money and shorter women."

Chary Jones listened to this exchange with a look of resigned calm. McGann introduced Wexton as an acquaintance in whose career he was interested. "He worked his way up from a busboy," he said proudly. "It proves that anything is possible in America."

"Really?" Chary Jones said. "How inspiring." She smiled and then moved gracefully away to look at the Kathleen Rogers portrait.

Wexton jerked his head toward the bartender. "That's Hymie, my photographer. He's got a Leica under the bar. When they get plastered enough he'll start shooting."

"That's wonderful," McGann said. He was really impressed. "Where's the help Holton thought he was hiring?"

"We gave them the night off at triple time." There was a commanding cough behind them. Wexton said, "Here comes Counselor Jerk."

Holton had a light grip on the elbow of a willowy blonde. He gave Wexton a sharp look. "There are other guests, you know."

The reporter said, "Yes, sir," and moved on with his tray. Holton told the blonde, "Miss Mars, this is Mr. McGann, the detective who is going to find the murderer of poor Mr. Tompkins."

"How exciting," Miss Mars said languidly. Her black gown was cut so low in front that McGann was afraid to look. The fingers holding the cocktail glass were heavy with jewels. "This is really an amazing coincidence," she added with more interest. "My lahst picture was a murder mystery—'So Evil, My Eye.' I do hope you saw it."

McGann shook his head sadly. "My doctor has forbidden me to attend the cinema," he said. "The features are all right but the trailers are too exciting." Chary Jones came back and he introduced the women, who looked at each other with undisguised curiosity.

"I've seen a lot of your pictures, Miss Mars," Chary said. "I thought the one with Boyer was marvelous."

"Sweet," Miss Mars said. "Isn't she sweet, Amos?" Holton agreed that Miss Jones was definitely sweet. McGann squeezed Chary's arm and insisted that he be allowed to vote, too. He signaled imperiously to Wexton for fresh drinks and when the tray was brought said, "Keep these coming, my good man. This isn't Operation Sahara, you know."

"Right you are, sir," Wexton said. He added in a low tone, "Were you expecting to meet a Mr. Michael Finn here tonight?"

McGann eyed his drink with suspicion. "No, I wasn't," he said, "and he'd better not show up. I'll finish that job on his esophagus."

They drifted toward the center of the room where a blonde in a red dress was talking animatedly with a darkly handsome man. She reached up and rubbed her palm along his cheek and by the gesture McGann recognized Irma Nelson. When she turned he saw that her face was flushed and her eyes were unnaturally bright.

Irma seemed principally interested in Gladys Mars. She threw up a hand in exaggerated welcome. "Well, well, well," she said, "if it isn't Clara Kimball Young! How's everything on the old Essanay lot, Clara? How's Wally Reid?"

Gladys Mars smiled warmly. "Irma, dahling," she said, "The moment I saw you I said 'What's missing?' and now I know. Your tray, dahling Where *is* your tray?"

"If I had one—around your neck," Irma sniffed and turned her attention to Amos Holton. McGann could not tell whether she overlooked him by accident or design. The dark, handsome man to whom she had been talking came over close to him and held out his hand slyly as if offering a bribe. "My name is Spanish," he said. "Solly Spanish." The tone was warmly confidential. This was inside stuff. Spanish tilted his glistening black head toward a laughing group in the corner.

"These citizens kill me. How can they be like this? The man's dead, right? So they should tone it down a little, right?"

McGann introduced himself but he shrugged off the question. "A lot of men have told their friends to celebrate instead of mourn," he said. "This is the sort of blowout Tompkins would like. He must be here in spirit."

Spanish's eyes showed white as his gaze slid around the room. "Go easy on that stuff, will ya, chum? I mean let's stick to what we know for sure." He had half a Rob Roy left and he finished it at a gulp. A drop escaped to his chin, and he took a fine linen handkerchief from his breast pocket and dabbed at it.

"Okay," McGann said. "What do we know for sure?" Spanish had nervously replaced the handkerchief askew and McGann reached over casually with a forefinger and poked the white triangle farther down into the pocket. The movement told him what he had wanted to know—Spanish had a gun in a shoulder holster. "What I mean," McGann said, "is that while I don't believe in spiritualism exactly, one must always be prepared for all eventualities, mustn't one?"

"You said it, chum," Spanish agreed eagerly. An immaculate cuff flashed as he laid a hand across his breast. "Me, I'm just a New York boy trying to get along, right? No rough stuff. Everybody friends. Let me get you a drink."

"Thanks," McGann said. "Martini."

McGann got to say a few words to Chary Jones before Spanish came back with the drinks. The smoke in the room grew heavier; the beat of the music on "A Pretty Girl Is Like a Melody" was steady, insistent. McGann saw Hope Harmon in the corner demonstrating how she used to do the showgirl slink to that one in the Follies. She still had a beautiful figure.

Frazier Farwell was in the group watching her. He held a cigarette but no drink. McGann thought, Maybe he really meant 'never again.' A girl with bluish hair detached herself from the crowd and began to make her way across the room. McGann angled to head her off.

"Miss Rogers?"

She started and turned. She was wearing red-rimmed harlequin glasses but he could see that as in the portrait her eyes were big and sad. In her hand she held a long, red cigarette-holder. "Yes?"

He told her his name and she seemed to recognize it. "You could help me," he said ingratiatingly.

"Really?" The eyes behind the upturning glasses were alert with suspicion. "How?"

"Were you at home yesterday about six-thirty?"

"Six-thirty?" A pale hand fluttered to the blue ringlets. "Why . . . I believe so. Yes. I was getting ready to go out about that time."

"Splendid." McGann dropped his voice to a confidential level "I understand your bedroom windows are across the court from the Tompkins study. Did you notice any activity over here then?"

"Activity?" She looked about as if hoping that something would occur to provide an escape. Then, "Why should I be looking over here?"

McGann shrugged. "Quite accidentally, I mean. Or you might glance out to see what's with the weather. You know."

For a moment she stared silently. "Mr. McGann, when I am getting dressed to go out, my blinds are closed. See what you can make of that." She glided away.

McGann was still staring after her when Wexton came up. He was thinking of a lighted window that had gone dark the first time that he had glanced out of the Tompkins study to the building across the court.

McGann accepted a fresh drink and Wexton asked, "Anything doing?"

"Sure. The joint is jumping with clues. Quote me on that."

"I've learned one thing," Wexton said.

"What's that?"

"I can drink a cocktail with one hand and hold a whole trayful with the other. Never knew I had it in me."

"Just don't get too much of it in you and disgrace Local 802," McGann said.

When he brought out cigarettes, Wexton put the tray on a serving table and accepted one. The cocktails undoubtedly had something to do with the reporter's new recklessness. "If Holton says anything to me I'll file a demurrer right on his bald spot," he said. "He can carry it to the Supreme Court, too, but it won't look good there."

They stood partly hidden by the screen before the serving table. The wake which Tompkins had ordered for himself was beginning to hit its stride. A number of persons were crowded before the bar now. A couple had started to dance, barely moving on the thick rug. The guitar was taking fast breaks on "There'll Be Some Changes Made," apparently another number on the Tompkins personal hit parade.

Chary Jones was talking with Farwell now. He was leaning over her attentively, and whatever he was saying it made her laugh. Gladys Mars was dazzling three men, expertly switching from one to another, keeping them all dazedly hopeful.

McGann surveyed her gown from this safer distance. "I think we can eliminate her," he said. "She isn't hiding anything."

Hope Harmon had completed exposition of the showgirl slink and was doing a refined grind. A grinning fat man was urging her on, clapping out the rhythm.

"Who's Two-ton?" McGann asked.

"That's Billy Besser," Wexton said. "When Hope's starring in a show he always has a supporting role. He supports her into the theater."

"A vital part," McGann agreed. He was looking for the red-head, Shirley Stanton. He saw her in a green dress over near the closed door leading into the study. Her white arms were up and she was throwing slow jabs at a hulking man who seemed about to burst the seams of a tight dinner jacket.

Several men and women were watching the performance. The men looked interested, the women bored. "Is that her fighter?"

"Yeah—'Hooker' Hunyak. She bought him with part of the dough Ronnie settled on her. She thinks she's going to win the heavyweight title with him."

"Is she?"

Wexton dropped the butt of his cigarette into the remains of somebody's highball. "I just hope she doesn't let one go," he said. "As the hired help I'd probably have to drag him out."

McGann straightened his bow tie. "I've got to circulate. You may follow as my cup bearer." He was reminded to take a new drink, pointed a warning finger at the white-jacketed reporter.

"Only a man in top condition should imbibe spirituous liquors. Remember that." He held the glass up to the light admiringly. "Top condition," he repeated.

Wexton finished one quickly and picked up his tray. "I was once a 97-pound weakling," he said. "Now I weigh 96 ½."

To McGann it seemed as if he were advancing into a layer of blue cirrus clouds as he moved forward. The heavy rug and the cocktails heightened the sensation of drifting dreamily. As he approached Gladys Mars and her trio of admirers, she flicked him with her roving glance. He bowed gallantly and when he looked up she was talking to the man on her right.

"One down," Wexton said behind him.

McGann ignored him. Chary Jones smiled warmly and Farwell raised a hand in greeting. When McGann held up the cocktail glass and arched his eyebrows, Farwell shook his head. "Moral fiber," he called. "Man of steel."

McGann paused briefly to approve the sinuous gyrations of Miss Harmon, and the fat man caught his eye. "Terrific, isn't she?" the fat man said. His plump face was shiny. McGann agreed that she was definitely terrific. He might have stayed longer but a hand plucked at his sleeve. It was Irma Nelson and her eyes were brighter than ever.

"Hello, Hawkshaw," she said. "How's the old slew of sleuth?" She rubbed her palm along his cheek. "Got rid of the disguise, eh?"

McGann assumed stern dignity. "I am now disguised as a gentleman," he said. Sully Spanish seemed intent on convincing a guest that the whole thing was too noisy for a wake, right? McGann patted Irma's cheek and told her that he was having red broadloom put on his fire-escape. There would also be a chromium handrail.

"No sale," Irma said. "Your coffee's lousy." She linked her arm cozily through his. "C'mon, Sherlock, I want to see what that fake redhead thinks she's doing."

Wexton was still trailing. When Irma noticed him, she helped herself to a stinger. "It brings out the real me," she explained. As they reached the group, "Hooker" Hunyak was demonstrating his famous punch. His eyes were surprisingly mild beneath beetling brows but the tuxedo was straining at every seam.

The men watched in frank admiration. Shirley Stanton patted his bulging bicep affectionately, as she might have soothed a horse. "We're working on a surprise for the next match," Shirley said. "'Hooker's' perfecting a new version of the old one-two."

Wexton was unimpressed. "The bum can't count that high," he whispered to McGann.

"Pipe down," McGann pleaded. "I've got to make friends here." He moved up with the blonde, said, "May I?" and felt the Hooker's other bicep. His expression was awed. "Sometimes Nature just shows off." He held out his hand and was careful to grasp Hunyak's steely fingers to forestall a nutcracker grip.

Shirley Stanton flung her flaming hair back from her shoulders and appraised him coolly. McGann noticed that she did not have a drink. He wondered if her eyes were really that green or whether it was the dress. Her stare was so calm that it was almost disconcerting, the pupils small, black and searching.

"You're the detective Ronnie called?"

Irma Nelson adjusted McGann's bow with a proprietary air. "Mickey is a wonderful detective," she said. "He can just look at your shoelace and tell right away if you forgot to tie it. He's elementary."

"*It's* elementary," McGann said. "Named after my old school." He signaled Wexton forward. "Can I offer you a libation or would you rather have a drink?" He wished Shirley Stanton would stop staring like that.

"No, thanks," she said. "I never touch it and Hooker drinks milk." She turned so that the others could not see her, half closed one eye and began to move slowly away.

McGann loosed Irma's arm and pushed her toward Hooker. "You two spar for a while," he said. "No biting."

The green dress was undulating ahead of him, halfway across the room. He started to walk faster, stopped short as a couple danced dreamily into his path. "My fault," McGann said. They ignored him. When he got around them, he saw that Shirley Stanton was no longer alone. A woman who touched a hand nervously to blue ringlets had stopped her.

From a dozen paces, McGann could see the sparks fly as Shirley Stanton and Kathleen Rogers faced each other. When he drew closer, it was the latter's voice that he heard first.

". . . as I'm standing here," Kathleen Rogers said. "But for you, he'd be alive today."

Shirley Stanton's spectacular bosom swelled dangerously but she gave no other indication of resentment. She said, "He never told me your company prolonged his life."

"I might have expected some such answer." The harlequin glasses flashed contemptuously. "Your nightclub Billingsgate does not intimidate me. I want you to know that I am aware of the methods you used to ensnare Ronnie—you . . . you cheap, designing—"

McGann expected the air momentarily to fill with red and blue hair but Kathleen Rogers, with what seemed a supreme effort, got hold of herself. She turned and flung past with an audible hiss, and he looked at Shirley Stanton.

"You deflated her," he said. "I could hear it."

"I'll snatch her bald," the redhead said, but her expression was puzzled. "What was that she said about Billingsley? Why drag Sherman into this?"

"They try to blame everything on cafe society," McGann said. They had moved on toward the Seyffert portrait when she suddenly touched his arm. The green eyes were fixed, boring into his. "There's something I want to tell you," she said. "I would never go to the police but I—"

"Wait a minute," McGann said, on a sudden hunch. He had been skeptical about the exceptional co-operation of the homicide bureau in allowing the murder mansion to be used so soon for such a gathering.

Now mention of the word "police" and the apparent proximity of some revelation, prompted a definite check. He moved to the side of the lighted portrait, which was hanging at a slight angle, and peered behind it.

As he expected, directly in the center he could make out a small black box—a "tin ear" in police parlance. He knew now that there must be one behind every other portrait, in all strategic parts of the room. Somewhere O'Callahan's men were getting a large earful, sifting the conversational wheat from the chaff for leads.

He shook his head warningly at Shirley Stanton. In front of the portrait he spoke directly to the concealed listening post. "Like I say, chum, O'Callahan is a big pig or my name ain't Solly Spanish, right?" He steered the redhead toward the center of the room. "Let's get away from here. They'll be peeking out through the eyes next like Bela Lugosi."

In the center of the room, comparatively safe from the delicate pickup microphones, she again faced him. McGann was struck by her marvelous calm in the den of mourners, who ran from jittery to hilarious. "It's only this—" she said.

"Hello, there," Frazier Farwell said. "Don't be so exclusive. This lady wants to dance with the guy what brung her."

Chary Jones looked embarrassed. "Don't say that. Mr. McGann escorted me only from a high sense of duty." Shirley Stanton looked helplessly at McGann, and he made a slight gesture for silence. He said, "In somebody else's lyrics—have you met Miss Jones?"

The women nodded, but not before Shirley Stanton had thrown a barbed look at Farwell. The guitarist thrummed a commanding chord and they turned to see Besser ponderously mounting a chair. "Ladies and gentlemen," he boomed, "may I now . . ."

He waited for the babble to subside. It swelled instead. "Ladies and gentlemen," he paused . . . "SHADDUP!" The smile on his shiny face was disarming. They shaddup. He leaped into the lull, holding his glass high. "A toast to our host wherever he is—a fine fellow and party-giver without peer—Ronnie Tompkins!"

An approving murmur swept the crowd. Glasses rose in tribute. McGann noticed that Shirley Stanton, having no glass, had folded her hands placidly. Chary Jones barely touched the glass to her lips. Farwell looked uneasy.

Besser was speaking again. "Attorney Holton has asked me to say that he has a surprise for you in the next room Kindly walk, do not run, to the exit behind me and grab a seat. I thank you."

Voices mounted in speculation. Guests were moving toward the door leading into the study. McGann took Chary's elbow, and she glanced at him questioningly. "Here we go again," he said.

11

THEIR MASTER'S VOICE

They all strolled across the art gallery together. Shirley Stanton spoke directly to McGann. "I may not get another chance to see you tonight," she said. "I'd like to invite you over to Hooker's training camp. Some of the others will be there."

"Great," McGann said. Celebrants were around them now and there was warning in his eyes. "Open house for everyone? Where's Hooker working out?"

"Ma Handy's. That's in Unionville, New Jersey. We've got some exhibition bouts tomorrow afternoon."

McGann nodded. "Swell. Like nothing better. And to make Counselor Holton happy you can be giving me a little background on Ronnie." He spoke nonchalantly, asked Chary, "You don't model on Sunday, do you—halos or something?"

"No." She looked eagerly at the redhead. "May I?"

"Of course."

"I accept," Farwell said. "I love Jersey—the dreamy smoke on the swamps, the friendly natives, dawn over Kearny."

A flicker of annoyance touched the creamy brow. "But your public—"

"My public will have to be brave—braver than my sabbath sponsor anyway. He's withdrawn his snake oil ad and I've already dusted the studio."

They were entering the study. Both women seemed to have grown a shade paler. Chary said, "This is where it happened, isn't it?"

"Yes," McGann said, watching her reaction. "The bloodstain's under that throw rug."

She moved stiffly to a chair. Shirley Stanton's stolid gaze circled the room of death. "I don't like surprises," she said flatly. She glanced back toward the art gallery. "I don't like being hung up there with those other prizes, either. I'm used to better company."

Farwell said, "Excuse me, I promised to help Holton." McGann waited until Shirley Stanton was seated and then he stepped to the shadows at the side of the room.

They were coming in, moving sideways along the rows of chairs. Some still held drinks. A few joked and laughed but mostly now they seemed curious and a little baffled at the turn in the festivities.

Wexton sidled up to McGann. The reporter had shed the white waiter's jacket, and put on his own coat, apparently banking on anonymity in the gloom. They waited without speaking.

The rows were filled. Holton closed the door between art gallery and study and glided to the front on silent feet. From the wall safe he took a flat package in what looked like gray flannel, carefully unwrapped it and handed a gleaming black record to Farwell.

With expert touch, the disc jockey slipped the recording to the turntable, made quick adjustments on the automatic mechanism. The audience was watching in silent wonder. Farwell pressed a button and stepped back. At the same moment, Holton extinguished all lights except a lamp that shown on the glistening machine.

There was a subdued hum.

"*Good evening,*" Ronnie Tompkins said. He chuckled. "*You weren't expecting me tonight, were you? But you know I'd rather die than miss a party . . .*"

The smooth voice filled the room, pinning them in their seats. McGann felt the hairs rise along his neck. A woman gasped and then they were leaning forward, deathly still.

"*At one time or another, all of you meant something rather special to me. You were grifters mostly, playing 'Good Time Ronnie' for what was in it. But don't look like that. I wasn't fooled and I loved you for what you were.*"

Pale faces were waxy in the reflected light, eyes fixed fascinated on the machine. The suave, unctuous voice held a note of weariness, of resignation.

"*Yes. You stood my insults if I stood you drinks—you took my name if a fortune went with it. You were for sale and I bought you. I threw you back so that no one would make the mistake of thinking I hoped to buy love. Believe me, I knew better than that.*"

A rustle ran through them like a chill wind over dead leaves.

"*Murderers!*" He seared them with it. "*You don't like that, do you? But you are. Ah, yes, you are . . .*" McGann saw the fat man half rise from his chair as though stung, then sink back. He looked sideways at Wexton and the reporter had his mouth open as if being dropped in an elevator. "*Oh, I don't suppose you realized it but you killed a part of me every time you did what I hoped you wouldn't and knew you would.*"

He called them by name, and now he seemed to have regained the old-time ease, the gently bantering tone. "*Being of sound mind—more sound than you ever thought, my dears—I have some bequests to make. Can you wait?*"

Briskly, Tompkins enumerated. The portraits to a special room at the Metropolitan with funds for the addition of a trustee-dazzling wing. So much to the servants, the house to a nursery settlement.

"For each of my wives, and any bride-elect, one hundred thousand dollars. My attorney will notify others of remembrances. The remainder of my estate to underwrite the institute I have ordered . . .

"Go on, now, with your party, my friends and my loves." The low laugh was a benediction. *"I'm with you, you know. I'm here."*

Heavy silence followed the metallic click. Footsteps sounded in the hall. Kathleen Rogers lifted her face to the shadowed ceiling and her scream cut through the crash of a heavy hand on the door, the splintering of glass. They were on their feet, crying and shoving, and McGann was knifing his way through toward the window when the lights sprang up.

"Stand where you are!" O'Callahan thundered. The usually pink face was beet-red, the white eyebrows bristled. "Where is he?" he demanded. "Where—"

"Here he is, Inspector." A bluecoat shoved Solly Spanish back through the gaping window. "He was flying down the fire-escape like Satan himself. And a cannon in his hand."

"Aha!" O'Callahan lumbered across the room, shoved his face into Spanish's panic-filled countenance. "A powder you're taking, eh? Well, take one with us. You and me will have a nice long talk."

Spanish's lips twisted but no sound emerged. Irma Nelson elbowed her way to his side, whirled on the inspector. "Why don't you leave him alone? He didn't do anything!"

"Maybe you'd like to come along?"

"Maybe I would."

"All right." O'Callahan nodded toward the door. "Both of them," he told the bluecoat. The cop and Spanish went first, Irma next. O'Callahan looked after them. "Pigs, is it?" he said. He swept the transfixed celebrants with a stern eye. "Why don't you people go home?" he said. "It's Sunday." He followed the others out.

McGann found Wexton sidling toward the door. The reporter's eyes glistened. "What a story," he said. "I may get a two dollar raise out of this."

"Drop by my place after you phone."

They were all suddenly sober. Holton was holding a glass of water for Kathleen Rogers, who was seated but still trembling. The celebrants milled about talking in low tones and gradually drifted out.

The lawyer mopped his gleaming pate when he stopped beside McGann. "Good Lord," he said, "I carried out my promise to Tompkins but what a mess." He shook his head, then smiled at what seemed a comforting thought. "I'm certainly glad I thought to bar the press."

"Absolutely," McGann said.

12

THE SQUARED CIRCLE

The convertible glided smoothly under McGann's hand, ignoring the crooked stones of Seventh Avenue. Sunday had come up with warmish autumn haze, now in the afternoon they were glad for the breeze. Chary Jones beside him on the red leather seat had a bright bandana around her dark head.

Farwell and Dink Wexton were quiet in the back. McGann swung right at the entrance to the Holland Tunnel and paid the uniformed guard. The cash register rang behind them and then they were humming through the tunnel, tile walls streaming past.

They emerged among the boxlike buildings of Jersey City and Wexton leaned forward. "Just pull over if you'd like me to say a few words on the political situation."

"What's the matter?" McGann said. "Tired of fresh air already?"

"Go ahead," Chary said. "If they put you in jail I'll bake you a cake with a file in it."

Wexton pretended to consider it. "How will I get the cake open?" he asked. Farwell suggested that it could be slipped unnoticed into the rock pile. Chary Jones said that the offer was withdrawn and they could all rot in jail before she raised a finger.

They rushed over the magnificent arch of the skyway with the smoke-smudged Jersey meadows spread out below. Chary Jones held a carmined thumb against the dashboard lighter, pressed the glowing coil to a cigarette. McGann asked, "How does it feel to be rich?"

"I like it." Her half-closed eyes were on the road unreeling before them. "Who doesn't?"

"I guess they can all use it—probably most of them blew what Ronnie had given them before. Even so, I heard Harmon say she'd give half of it to have him back."

Farwell hunched forward in the rear seat, talking loudly against the wind. "What's this institute Ronnie mentioned he was leaving so much to?"

"I asked Holton that," McGann said. "It'll be announced officially tomorrow so it's no dark secret. He left it to finance a marriage clinic."

"A what?"

"An institute on marriage—anti-divorce counsel and that sort of thing. With the national divorce rate one in three, Ronnie thought something should be done about it."

Farwell snorted. "That tears it," he said. "Ronnie of all people. I've heard everything now."

Chary looked back. "I don't know. I think it's exactly like him. He'd do something good if he could put a strange twist on it. No—I'm not surprised."

Wexton had no comment and appeared to be dozing. They turned off the skyway past Newark airport, glimpsing a silver giant swinging in the sun. When they reached "Ma" Handy's training camp at Unionville, dozens of cars were parked in the gravel area.

Shirley Stanton came out to meet them. She was wearing a tight green sweater and maroon slacks. Wexton eyed her approvingly. "Any time you want to practice clinching, let me know," he said.

"Back to your corner, lightweight," the redhead said. She smiled at Farwell and McGann and linked her arm through

Chary's. "It's wonderful that you got here. Come on in and meet 'Ma.'"

"Ma" Handy was plump with beautiful ankles and black hair pulled back into a knot. She hailed them in a voice like a Diesel exhaust, and sized up McGann speculatively. "If you'd like to pick up a couple of bucks," she said, "we're short of sparring partners. Hooker's knocked out two already this afternoon."

"I'd be glad to," McGann said, "only I mislaid my killer instinct. Don't you need a timekeeper or something?"

Wexton shadow-boxed, fancy Dan. "I'm your man. I use gloves with built-in towels. Where's the victim?"

He drew a withering glance. "One thing I hate to see is the result of a misspent life." She threw out a powerful arm and pulled him to her queen-size bosom. "What you need every morning are a couple of Indian clubs."

Wexton struggled loose. "What I need every morning," he said, "are a couple of Canadian clubs."

Shirley Stanton led the way to the rear. They could hear the drubbing of a light bag, the plop of heavy gloves. A score of spectators, mostly men, were sitting on folding chairs or standing around a ring set up under the trees. Two welterweights were pounding each other industriously, their bodies shiny with sweat.

A skinny colored boy was rapping the light bag in tricky rhythms. Off to one side, Hooker Hunyak was skipping rope, moving his big-shouldered body with remarkable ease. He barely lifted his feet, knees stiff, from the ground.

"That's as close as I ever came to being a professional fighter," Farwell said. "Skipping rope. When I got through with that I took up jacks."

"Did you win?" Chary wanted to know.

"Licked every girl in the neighborhood."

"Some of the other people drove over," Shirley told McGann, "but I guess we won't see Irma and Solly."

McGann explained that Spanish was still busy trying to evade a Sullivan law charge for carrying a weapon. Irma Nelson had been released after three hours and six repetitions of her explanation for the presence of her doll pillow in the mansion.

A shout escaped the crowd as one of the welterweights landed a sharp blow. McGann had stepped a bit apart with the redhead. She turned and laid a hand on his arm in that curiously calm manner. Her eyes held him in a fixed stare. "You know I don't believe that story," she said. "I think I can tell you who killed Ronnie and why."

"Who did it?"

The sun setting behind her made a blood-red halo of her spectacular hair. "This isn't going to be easy for me, believe that," she said. "It involves a confession of my own." She hesitated. "I think the others are watching us."

"Forget about them."

"No. Look. I'm staying in that cottage down the road." He could see white clapboards through the trees. "We'll serve a buffet supper later, and show some old fight movies. I'll get away and you see me there."

"Better not to—" McGann began but she was already moving back among the crowd. McGann recognized several of Tompkins' men friends who had been at the cocktail wake, found himself next to the pudgy Besser and Hope Harmon as Hunyak climbed into the ring followed by a giant Negro.

"Hello, there." The fat man's tone was cordial. "I don't know your name but I remember seeing you last night." McGann told him his name. Besser said, "Dear, this is Mr. McGann—Miss Harmon."

"Charmed," McGann said. "I was admiring your dancing."

"Don't mention it," Hope Harmon said. There were tired lines about her once fine eyes. "I don't even want to think about it." The fat man winked. "She's a little stiff today. Come to think of it, she was a little stiff last night, too."

"Bill!" She pulled her arm away crossly. "Must you?"

"Awfully nice knowing you," McGann said, and edged away. Hunyak and the Negro had begun sparring, the latter ponderous, using his superior weight to crowd the challenger. He landed a looping right on Hooker's headpiece and the spectators cheered.

"Hit 'im again, Haile!" a woman yelled.

The Negro's arms, in close, were working like ebony pistons. Hunyak bounced back. His heavy brows were protected by the thick leather headgear but his eyes still showed that gentle reserve.

Again the sparring partner moved in. Hunyak tapped him high on the chest with a left, drove a short jarring right to the midsection, then detonated his left hook. It flashed out viciously, a white arc against the chocolate backdrop. Even with the outsize gloves it sounded like a sledgehammer on an orange crate. Blood spurted from the Negro's nose and mouth. He wavered.

The crowd sucked in its breath, and then McGann understood why it had seemed against Hunyak from the start. Hooker measured the faltering man with his innocent eyes. It didn't seem possible but he appeared ready to follow up his advantage.

McGann looked around for the referee. After all, it was only a sparring match and the man was hurt though still on his feet. The referee didn't seem interested. A ringsider started to say, "Why don't—" The Negro pawed the air vaguely and the second hook went off.

The smack was wet, spewing crimson and the big man went down in sections like a dynamited smokestack. A woman near McGann looked the other way and a man groaned. He could feel the crowd sicken. His gaze swung to the others to see how they were taking it. Chary Jones appeared transfixed with horror.

Revulsion seemed to have taken command of Farwell, too, but Dink Wexton surveyed the drama with amiable calm.

The seconds were leaping into the ring. Hunyak did not linger to help. He pulled off his headgear, waited only enough for a black robe to be thrown over his shoulders, then clambered out. Just before stepping down, he turned his guileless smile on the crowd. They were all silent as Hunyak walked through, then sounds of anger and disgust crackled after him.

McGann sought out the others on the fringe of spectators. He told the reporter, "I think there's another opening on the sparring staff."

"I'd rather walk into a propeller," Wexton said. All disdain of Hunyak's potency had vanished. "If he even looks at me I'll start doing roadwork."

They were helping the dazed boxer out. He patted broken lips clumsily with his taped hands. Chary had roused to indignation. "If that's a manly art," she said, "I've finally found a reason to be glad I'm a woman. I can't understand Shirley—"

"It's not always like that," McGann said. "The referee should have stepped in. It's that second blow that does the damage."

Ma Handy charged down upon them with appalling vigor. "Shirley tells me you're all staying for supper and the movies," she boomed. "That's swell. We've got a big buffet and Dempsey-Carpentier and some others."

They watched several exhibition bouts and McGann won five dollars from Wexton. He looked in vain for Shirley Stanton. He was surprised to catch a glimpse of Kathleen Rogers, who strolled out with a tanned young man. She gazed about, as if looking for someone, then was lost in the crowd.

It was getting dark when the final bell rang. They went in to the buffet. McGann saw that a large room had been fitted up for the fight films. He excused himself to Chary Jones and Wexton.

"I've got a little errand. See you in the showers." He told Chary, "Don't let him talk you into betting on Carpentier when they start that film. He's old enough to remember how it came out."

She smiled. "Don't worry. I know all about sports, too. I'll pick Didriksen to beat Louis any time."

"Fine, fine. Then I don't have to guard your interests."

It was dark when he stepped outside. There was a thin mist on the leather seat of the convertible. On the windshield, the mist made the camp lights glow large and yellow like the candles on a Christmas card.

He eased behind the wheel. The motor caught quickly, then he was threading his way to the main road. There he turned right, ran swiftly through the gears and sped at a steady pace toward a roadhouse he remembered from the drive in.

It proved to be farther than he had expected. A red neon sign spelled out Dirty Danny's. He went into the long low building where a wave of stale smoke and sour beer hit him. Four men playing shuffleboard did not look up but a few heads turned at the bar. A juke-box about the size and color of the Roxy marquee was thumping out "Twelfth Street Rag."

McGann told the bartender, "Scotch and water," and slid over a five-dollar bill. "I'd like some small change, please."

He took the change and the drink into the telephone booth. The juke-box was muffled through the closed door. He found Amos Holton's home number in the notebook he took from his pocket—a Butterfield exchange. He dialed the operator and gave it to her.

After a moment she said, "Deposit twenty cents, please." The dimes rang out four cheap chimes. Then the Holton phone was ringing. He held the throbbing receiver a little away from his ear and sipped the Scotch. The New York phone didn't answer and he flashed her. "Would you mind ringing that again, please?"

"I will try the number ay-gain, sir," she said.

It was no good. Just for the record, he tried Holton's office and drew another blank. He told the operator, "If my dimes aren't worn out, give me Rector 2-3515. This I know will answer."

She said, "I weel try to get them for you, sir."

The Manhattan office of the FBI answered. McGann got an agent he knew, asked, "Is there anything in the file on Louis Hunyak, also known as Hooker?"

His Scotch was almost gone before the agent came back on the phone. There was a thin dossier on Hunyak—native of Yugoslavia, brought to the United States at the age of three . . . now a citizen . . . drafted September 1942 . . . discharged from service April 1943 for the good of the same.

"What did he do?" McGann wanted to know. "Tie cannons in knots in a fit of pique?"

Hunyak, he was told, had been in just enough scrapes to get thrown out without drawing the guardhouse. No, he had not been in any other trouble. As for the Tompkins affair, if McGann personally wanted to confess over the phone his former colleague would be happy to take the confession and arrange his surrender.

"I ain't talkin'," McGann said.

He hung up and was about to step from the booth when the phone rang sharply. He lifted the receiver. "Deposit fifteen cents for overtime," the operator said. She sounded suspicious. "You got me," McGann said, "and I was almost over the border, too." Her "*Thank* you" cut through the vibrating bells.

He put the empty glass on the bar and drove back to the training camp. The fight films were on when he reached the porch and he looked in at the crowd. It was too dark to see anyone clearly. He went back to the car, took a flashlight from the glove compartment and started along the trail to the cottage Shirley Stanton had pointed out.

13
BUT NO AWAKENING

McGann's flashlight stabbed along the narrow trail. He could see a light in the cottage window. A few last insects cricked in the brush, a mournful farewell to summer. He went up the four steps to the porch and saw that the door was half open.

He snapped off the flashlight and tapped it on the wood of the screen door. There was no answer. He rapped again, called, "Miss Stanton!"

The cottage was utterly silent. McGann opened the screen door and stuck his head inside. "Hello," he called, "are you—"

Shirley Stanton was at ease in a low chair, her legs in the maroon slacks stretched out on a flowered hassock. Her eyes were closed, the long lashes lying on her flawless skin and the brilliant hair billowed about her. A magazine was on her lap.

McGann coughed, pushed the screen open and let it slam. The green sweater swelled in a torturously long, slow breath. "Sorry to come barging—" McGann began loudly. Something about the incredible length of the breath she took made him walk over to her.

His fingers closed on the soft wool of her shoulder and he shook her sharply. "Wake up!" She did not stir and he shook her again, hard. The seconds ticked off an eternity—five, ten, fifteen. The sweater started on another breath.

McGann dropped to his knees and shoved the glowing flashlight in her face. The lovely features were marble clean and cool in the bright circle.

With his left thumb he pushed back her eyelid. The green eye was rolled slightly upward and he had to get hold of the lid with thumb and forefinger and lift it. It stared back at him as always, only this time the pupil was the tiniest pinpoint possible.

He had seen the effects of morphine before but never quite so pronounced. For a moment he stood irresolute. If Shirley Stanton was fighting a slight overdose, an alarm would set off a chain of explosive trouble for her.

If not—if it were more than that—she might never get to tell him what she had called him here to reveal. He timed her breaths. Not more than four a minute. This was definitely coma. He looked about swiftly, walking into the small bedroom, but there was no phone.

There would be one at the camp and no need now for the secrecy which had sent him to the roadhouse booth. McGann stepped quickly to the door and collided jarringly with a figure on the dark porch. Taut reflexes had his free hand on the man's neck before he realized that he had reached out.

"Damn it to hell, Mac, let go of my neck," Dink Wexton said as soon as he could. He seemed really mad. His thin face was twisted in the light of the flash, and he was pressing his throat gingerly. "There's nothing left of my Adam's Apple but the core."

McGann's voice was not friendly. "What are you doing up here?" He kept the light on Wexton. "How long have you been here?"

The reporter stared, the eyes wide above their brownish shadows. "Hey," he said, "what's eating you? I just came up."

"Why?"

Wexton shrugged. "I could say it's a free Jersey but I won't. I saw you come up on the porch and look in at the movie."

The detective's tone softened. "So you came along to see what you could see?"

"Something like that. What's up?"

McGann told him. "I'm pretty sure it's morphine poisoning. She's in a bad way. Get a doctor and an ambulance and tell Ma Handy but don't bring the whole gang. I'll wait."

"O.K.," Wexton said. "Let me borrow the light. I tried to knock over a tree coming up here."

McGann watched the light bobbing back toward the main building, then turned and went back in. The lovely figure rested softly, easily against the chair. Slim fingers were curled lightly about the magazine in her lap.

He went over and looked at it. It was a copy of "The Ring" and was open at Page 10. Hooker Hunyak posed mildly on the page, his lethal fists extended, his expression almost spiritual.

McGann took it gently from her listless hands and put it on a table. For a moment he thought that she had stopped breathing altogether. He held in mid-motion, watching the green sweater. With infinite weariness Shirley Stanton accepted a life-giving breath. He took her polo coat from a chair and put it over her gently.

The detective's gaze roamed the room. There was an ash-stand on the redhead's left and in it three cigarettes had been crushed out. The ends of two were smeared with lipstick and were only half smoked. The third was clean but smoked down to less than an inch. He picked them up and slipped them into his coat pocket.

He went into the little kitchen, finding the cord to an over-head dome and pulling it on. Yellow light flooded over a small sink, a two-burner kerosene range, a camp table and chairs. There was a coffee-pot on the stove and he went over and felt it. It was still warm.

Two cups stood on the kitchen sink. One was almost empty with just a drying brown ring in the bottom. The other contained about half an inch of dark liquid. There was a faintly acrid odor when he put his nose to it.

Footsteps rushed up to the porch as he took a tentative taste. The coffee was thick, shudderingly powerful. Ma Handy slammed in. "My God," she said. "What's the matter? What is it?"

"Our girl friend got too much of something," McGann said. "I think it's morphine. Did you know she was an addict?"

"No." She moved her heavy body on the slim ankles, looking down at the still face. "We called an ambulance It'll have to come from Elizabeth." She laid two fingers on the limp wrist. "Her pulse is awfully slow. Isn't there something we can do for her?"

McGann stood beside her, holding the coffee cup and staring at the redhead. "If she stops breathing altogether we can give her artificial respiration. That's about all, though, except keep her warm until the ambulance gets here."

He pulled over a chair. "You sit here and watch her. I want to look around some more."

"What for?"

"Notes for one thing. If she took an overdose on purpose there should be some around. This will be a police matter, you know. If she was deliberately given an overdose I'd like to find out how."

She flicked a capable hand. "Hop to it."

There was nothing in the bedroom resembling a farewell note. An alligator purse was lying on the bed and he opened it and pawed through it. An unopened pack of Camels, a lipstick, keys, handkerchief. In the purse compartment some bills and loose change.

"She's still breathing," Ma Handy said. "Find anything?"

"No." McGann had left the coffee cup on the table beside the magazine He picked up the latter and shook it out but nothing dropped from between the pages. Riffling through it, he could see no marginal notations.

"Better see if there's anything in her pockets," he said. "If she pulls through this, she'll thank us for keeping them dark."

After a minute, Ma Handy said, "Only a book of matches. From the Chanticler."

"Let me have them," McGann said. He put them into his pocket with the recovered cigarette butts. In a kitchen cabinet he found a brown paper bag and a couple of small empty jars with tops. He put coffee from the pot in one and scratched the top. He poured what was left in the cup into the other. He shoved both jars and the second cup with its brown ring into the bag just as the throaty moan of the ambulance sounded near the camp.

"Thank God," Ma Handy said. "Here they come. I told your little friend to stay there and show them the way up."

"Good," McGann said. "There's nothing else here." From the porch he saw the red eye of the ambulance winking through the trees. Lights were going up in the main camp building and people were coming out on the porch. Flashlights advancing along the trail grew brighter.

Wexton was first and directly behind him were two white-coated attendants carrying a rolled-up stretcher. McGann held the door open and they stepped aside to let an interne enter first. He was a dark and serious young man.

Almost while they were opening the stretcher he completed his triad examination—pulse, pupils, respiration. "Drugged, all right," he said. "Take her."

The door slammed and Hooker Hunyak stood in the room, massive, menace in his hunched shoulders. His gaze touched her tenderly, moved to the others. "What are ya trying to do?" he said. "Why is she like that?"

The attendants ignored him, lifting the limp form and her bright head tilted back from the lovely curve of her throat. McGann walked over. "She's sick," he said. "She has to go to the hospital."

Slowly the wide eyes took him in. Instead of standing squarely, Hunyak instinctively slid his left foot forward. "No she doesn't," he said.

McGann watched the left shoulder. "It's the only chance to save her life. You want them to save her, don't you?"

The attendants had lifted the stretcher. They stood waiting. The interne adjusted a blanket. Hunyak backed reluctantly. His words were heavy, addressed to McGann. "Nothing better happen to her then, understand?"

McGann nodded to the interne and the attendants. The stretcher started out. He showed his credentials to the young doctor. "I'd like to ride with her. Anything she says can be very important."

"I guess it's O.K."

McGann held the paper bag with its jars and cup down near his side. He told Wexton, "Stick near me." They walked along the narrow trail directly behind the interne. The crowd from the camp stood in a silent and curious ring back of the ambulance.

While the stretcher was being loaded, McGann went to his car and put the bag in the glove compartment. He locked it. Then he took the ignition key from the ring and handed it to Wexton. "You got a driver's license?"

"Yes."

"I'm going to ride in the ambulance. You bring Chary and Frazier. I'm sticking with the Stanton girl but I'm not sure how long it'll be before we know one way or the other."

"I'll follow you to the hospital."

"Yes. If any of you want to go back to New York you can get the Pennsylvania at the Elizabeth station. Or wait if you'd like."

"All right."

The stretcher was loaded. McGann walked over and swung up on the rear step, into the dim, warm interior. They had transferred Shirley Stanton to a heavier, chrome-trimmed stretcher-bed on wheels.

The interne was on the long seat beside her, his fingers on her pulse. Another low moan and they swung around slowly toward the road. Through the glass of the side McGann saw Hooker Hunyak posed stolidly, his arms heavy at his sides.

Wide tires and special springs floated them over the highway bumps. The warning wail sounded as they slipped past intersections. Neon signs wheeling by cast garish reflections across the peaceful features of the sleeping girl.

"How is she, Doc?"

"Deep," the interne said. "Deep as they can get without—"

After a bit, "There isn't even much you can do in the hospital, is there?"

"Watch and hope. Keep them warm."

McGann thought of the art gallery in the Tompkins study.

"She was Shirley Stanton, cigarette girl . . . out of this world . . . completely . . . I proposed instantly . . ." Green eyes staring fixedly. "I think I can tell you who killed Ronnie and why . . . it isn't easy . . . they're watching us . . ."

Country blackness gave way to brightly-lighted streets. Now the siren was on almost continuously, and cars and buses pulled over before it. They were turning into a side driveway and a sign with a light behind it said, "Emergency."

They wheeled her along the quiet corridor and the elevator hummed them upward. McGann waited in the hall for a few minutes and then the nurse came out and said, "All right." Shirley Stanton's hair was even more violent against the white pillow, a startling background for the immobile features.

The interne stayed for a long time. When he went out, a nurse came in and stood watch. They slipped hot water bottles under the blankets. Shirley Stanton was a marble statue that had toppled from a pedestal.

A man who wore a gray fedora came to the door and crooked a finger at McGann. He walked into the hall. The man showed a Union County detective's badge. McGann brought out his credentials again and told him briefly of finding her. "I don't know about relatives," he said. "Ma Handy will call them, if there are any around here, and then come over."

"I know Ma," the county man said, "and I knew something about this girl's connections with Tompkins. I'll wait with you. Maybe two will listen better than one."

Shirley Stanton's lovely lips never opened. At 11:21 P.M. she was really out of this world.

14

OVER THE RIVER

McGann walked out, past the stunned Ma Handy, the stricken fighter. He felt intolerably weary. As often as he had looked upon death, the tragedy of the young and lovely weighed heavily upon him.

"Better not to—" had been his last words to Shirley Stanton. She had walked away into the crowd, not letting him finish. He would have said "—not to put it off."

But she had put it off. Now she was dead, and her secret was dead. What was it that she had wanted to reveal? "They're watching us—" Who they? "It involves a confession on my part?" What confession? He turned it over and over in his mind.

He stepped off the elevator into the hospital lobby. Wexton was there and three other men, apparently local reporters. They immediately came up to him. "She's gone," McGann said. He told them the time. "She never came to."

"Is it suicide or murder or what?" Wexton asked.

"There were no notes," McGann said. He had been for hours without a cigarette and now he lighted one, inhaled deeply. "That's all I can tell you. There'll be an autopsy first thing to-morrow. We'll all know more then."

They were turning away. "Let me phone this in," Wexton said. "Chary's in the car half a block to the left as you go out. Farwell finally took the Pennsy back."

117

"We'll wait for you."

She was huddled down in the corner of the front seat, and raised a fearful face when he came up. Her eyes asked the question. He shook his head. "There wasn't anything they could do."

"Oh!" There was a world of pity in the muffled cry. She sat staring straight ahead, and McGann went around and slid behind the wheel. After a while he said, "It's just about the kindest, easiest death there is. They never wake up."

Light from the street lamp etched her profile against the black building. She didn't turn. He thought of what he had just said and of the pillow under Ronnie Tompkins' head. He sat smoking quietly until Dink Wexton trotted up.

The reporter climbed into the back. "Let's get out of here," he said. "I'd rather take my chances in Manhattan."

They rode in silence. McGann turned off the skyway and drove into Hoboken. "Mind taking the ferry back?" he asked. "I could use a river breeze."

"I'd like that," Chary murmured.

"Go by way of submarine for all I care," Wexton said. "I'm going to sleep."

They rattled over the planks and joined the line of cars moving into the yawning center of the Barclay Street ferry. They stopped, bumper to bumper, about the middle of the boat. Wexton slid down in the seat and tilted his hat over his eyes in sudden relaxation.

Up on the bridge a bell rang. They cast off to rattling chains and clanking winches. The whole ferry shook as the paddies churned and then they were gliding into the blackness of the Hudson.

"Let's go up front," McGann said.

"All right."

They left Wexton slumped in the back seat and edged their way along the cars parked ahead of them. Over on the right the rail was dark and empty and they leaned on it. The river was ink, except where the ferry churned up white spume. Far across the river glowed lights of the sleepless city and down the bay the tiny lady raised her torch.

The breeze felt good on McGann's forehead. They were close together in the dark and he was surprised to feel her link her arm through his. "I'm afraid," she said simply.

"Yes."

"I don't think she killed herself. She wasn't—"

"Don't say she wasn't the kind," McGann said. "Almost everybody's the kind under certain circumstances. But I don't think she killed herself either."

She seemed to think about that while the ferry made a long slow swing to the left. Up ahead a busy little tug huffed by with a string of barges and the ferry hooted warningly.

Chary said, "And it wasn't accidental either?"

"The autopsy will show just how much morphine was taken and then we can judge. But she went so fast I'm sure it was a great amount. They can linger for days with a slight overdose, you know."

A tremor seemed to run through her and her arm tightened. "But how—"

McGann thought of the coffee cup and of the jars in the locked glove compartment of the car. "They'll find out," he evaded.

She pressed the point. "And—and why? Why Shirley?"

She had said, *I think I can tell you who killed Ronnie . . . they're watching us . . .*"

But McGann said softly, "I don't know."

Manhattan slipped toward them, skyscrapers rearing into the darkness, lights splashing along the docks. Slowly, Chary withdrew her arm, shoved both hands deep into the pockets of her coat. McGann appeared to notice the withdrawal no more than he had remarked the original overture. He could see her face plainly now, drawn in its loveliness, the lips slightly parted.

He spoke lightly. "I'm going to suggest something but I want you to take it strictly as a sensible measure. After what's happened it's silly to tell you not to be alarmed, but let's say don't be any more alarmed."

Her eyes already had begun to widen at his words. "What? What is it?"

"I'm going to dump Wexton. Then I'll take you home and you pack a bag. I want to leave you at a hotel and I want to be the only one who knows where you are."

She nodded. "Anything you say."

The ferry was heading for the slip. They walked back quickly. They had just slammed the car doors when the ferry pushed heavily against the pilings and lurched back toward the center of the slip with a mad throbbing of reversed engines.

Wexton sat up scowling. "This is the noisiest, movingest boudoir I ever curled up in. My insults to the captain."

"You're home," McGann said. "Be glad. Wake up smiling."

Engines raced in the long line as the metallic clanking told of winches tightening. Then they were rolling off into the wide sweep of West Street. McGann headed uptown. He said over his shoulder to Wexton, "You want to go to your office or some place, don't you?"

"Since you put it that way," Wexton said, "I do."

They dropped him at an Eighth Avenue subway station and drove to Chary's place. "I'll come up," McGann said.

"Four floors and no elevator," she warned.

He waved airily. "Tomorrow, Mt. Everest. Just so long as you're below timberline."

She packed swiftly while he waited in the front room. He heard her talking in low tones to someone in the bedroom. She came out with an overnight case and he took it. When they were in the hall she said, "I told Mom I was going to stay with a girl friend to go on a special job."

"Good."

She laughed excitedly. "Where am I going? Or will I be blind-folded?"

"I'll tell you in the car."

"I'm sorry. I keep forgetting that walls have ears." She looked about as they reached the landing. "These could stand washing, too."

When they were heading east, he said, "I have in mind a quiet, secluded little nook for you. The Waldorf. An ideal hideout if there's anything to that purloined letter dodge."

"Oh, wonderful!" She seemed exhilarated, the earlier fright and depression temporarily forgotten. "Week end at the Waldorf! Come to think of it, I can afford it, too."

"If you can't," McGann said, "Holton can. When this is over, I'm going to spend a Month at the Mills."

He pulled in at the Park Avenue side and the doorman took the case. When they were going up the steps into the main lobby he told her that she might as well register in her own name. "After all, Mary Jones is practically anonymous."

She glared in bogus indignation. "For a man who was named after a truck you are getting on dangerous ground, Mr. Mack. That name is my cross."

McGann almost said, "Any time you'd like I'll change it for you" but decided against such a strong statement. Instead he left her seated and approached the desk. He showed the clerk his card and mentioned the name of a member of the house detective staff. "He'll vouch for me."

The clerk studied his precise cuffs for a moment. "We're very crowded. However—" He pulled a celluloid-covered sheet from a file and scanned it. "Yes. I think we can put the young lady up." He placed a card before the fountain-pen stand. "If you'll have her register, please."

McGann signaled and Chary walked over. She signed her name and the clerk looked at it, almost raising his eyebrows at this crude bit of subterfuge. McGann grinned and she tapped the toe of a black pump on the marble floor.

"Thank you, Miss—ah—Jones," the clerk said. A bellboy leaped at his signal. The clerk gave him the number of a seventeenth floor room. McGann went up with them, waited until the bellboy was through with his act, and tipped him. The bellboy left and they stood at the door.

"I'll call you tomorrow," McGann said. "Don't tell anyone where you are until we see how things stand. The party is getting way too rough. Just try to play happy hermit and wait until you hear from me."

He held out his hand. Her fingers were firm and cool. "Thank you, Mack." Her smile was light, friendly. "I'll try to put up with the place for as long as you say."

"Well—goodnight."

She drew him gently forward and laid fragrant lips against the corner of his mouth. "Goodnight, dear," she said and closed the door.

He stood staring at the brass numerals on the dark panel. Then he turned and walked slowly to the elevators. After a moment the light flashed and the door slid back. "Up?" said the operator, looking at McGann. He looked again, "Down?"

"Who cares?" McGann said and got on.

He walked through the empty lobby of the office building and signed the night watchman's book. His green-shaded lamp made a small pool of light over the blotter and he set the jars and cups down in it. He pushed his hat to the back of his head and sat down and placed the three cigarette butts and the book of matches in the circle of light.

Strong brown fingers pushed at the black-tipped bits. The lipstick on the matching pair was a warm, rosy shade, a hint of orange perhaps. He remembered the lipstick in Shirley Stanton's purse—Schiaparelli's "Inferno." It was hers, all right.

He took an enlarging glass from the drawer and studied them closely, turning them over slowly. Under the glass he could see more plainly the irregular labial impressions. He could also see under the bright smear the dotted-out letters PM&C. That would be Philip Morris. She had had an unopened pack of Camels in her purse.

The other cylindrical bit still contained the top of a blue M in the middle. A Camel. But the tip was clean. There was not even the light brown stain where the paper would have been wet. McGann thought of a cigarette holder. He sighed. That could throw the whole thing out. It was one of the main drawbacks of such clues.

He looked at the book of matches. Chanticler. A night-club in the Oranges. It was half-empty—the matches pulled from the right-hand side. That would make Shirley Stanton right-handed. Easily checked anyway. Yet the ash-stand had been on her left. For the convenience of a guest?

"Nuts," McGann said. He leaned back and lit one of his own cigarettes from a packet that said "fresh up" with 7 up. He sat for a long time smoking and looking at the articles on the desk blotter. Then he dialed Holton's home, let it ring. There was no answer.

15
TATTLING TEST TUBES

On the way to the office next morning, McGann stopped off at a 39th Street chemical house and left the coffee cup and the jars. He knew the analyst in charge and asked for a quick report. "Just to make it easy," he said, "I'm looking for morphine."

"Call me this afternoon," the analyst said. "How you doing since you left Uncle?"

"Wonderful. I've got more mysteries than you've got solutions."

The chemist grinned, tapped brown-stained fingers on a jar. "There's a retort for that, but I wouldn't want to be precipitate. Catalysten to more?"

"Good God, not" McGann said. "I'm sorry I brought it up. I'll call you about two."

"Don't go away burning, Bunsen."

McGann seldom used his car in Manhattan, preferring taxis for short trips. He had kept this one waiting and now he went on to his 42nd Street office. His secretary said, "Mr. Wexton called. He said he'd call again later."

"Thanks. Will you get me the medical examiner's office in Elizabeth?"

The report from New Jersey was concise and as expected. A total of 250 milligrams of morphine had been found in the brain and liver of ex-Mrs. Tompkins No. 6. It was a lethal dose and the direct cause of death. No other factors entered into it. Indications were that she had been employing morphine as a sedative for some time.

McGann asked, "By mouth or needle?"

"Mouth. There were no hypo scars."

He made rapid notes. Then he called the Waldorf and asked for Chary's seventeenth-floor room. When he heard a cautious "Hello?" he said, "Is this Miss—ah—Jones?"

"Oh, hello!" She sounded pleased. "How are things on earth?"

"Meaning you're in heaven, I hope."

"Nothing less. I have an Aladdin's lamp in this little gadget connected to room service. And I love being a hermit. Right now I'm sitting on the bed, wearing a fetching blue negligee and thinking of lifting those silver covers on the breakfast cart."

"Don't wear yourself out," McGann said. "But I'm glad you like the cave. I'll be seeing you."

"Call for an appointment."

He slipped his notebook into his inside coat pocket and told his secretary, "I'm going over to Holton's office. Be back by noon."

The law firm of Holton, Bolton, Durstine & Schwab was on lower Broadway. A dark-eyed, exotic-looking receptionist asked McGann to wait. She called an inner office, then stood up and smiled. She asked, "Will you follow me?"

"To the ends of the earth," McGann said.

"It's really not that far." She moved lithely before him, opened a frosted door. "I leave you here."

A pretty secretary guided him across a tastefully-appointed inner sanctum to the inmost. Holton was behind his desk and he looked up with his pale, undertaker's smile.

"Ah, good morning," Holton said. His thin fingers indicated a chair. "Sit down."

McGann offered the lawyer a cigarette which was declined. Holton lit a small, black cigar and held the light for the detective. McGann said, "I tried to call you last night. I suppose you've heard about Stanton?"

"Shirley Stanton? No, I haven't heard anything about her." Blue smoke curled around Holton's pallid dome. "I drove to the country yesterday and just came back this morning."

"She's dead," McGann said.

"Well," the lawyer said. "Dead, eh?" A bit of loose leaf seemed to annoy him and he spent a moment clipping it from the end of the cigar. "How'd she do it?"

"I don't think she did it."

"So?" The black eyes studied him meditatively. "Well, what do you think happened?"

McGann told him. He concluded, "I think the dose was too heavy to be accidental. I doubt suicide for several reasons."

"For instance?"

"In the first place, a woman almost never commits suicide without leaving a note. They seem to have some compulsion about it. I think a vain beauty like Stanton would have arranged a more theatrical setting for her final scene—a negligee in her Park Avenue penthouse rather than sweater and slacks in a Jersey fight camp."

Holton nodded. "Logical. And—"

"And she had a special reason for wanting to live for a while at least. She wanted to tell me who killed Ronnie Tompkins."

"Ahh." The sound escaped thinly from the drawn-back lips. "Ahh . . . she knew then?"

"She thought she did."

"But she had no opportunity to divulge her suspicions?"

McGann thought of the scene at the cocktail wake, the moments at the fight camp. "Something always intervened."

"What did she mean when she told you that it involved a confession on her part?" The lawyer leaned forward with a new display of interest. "Do you think that this is her way of confessing to Tompkins' murder?"

McGann said he didn't think so. He believed that the "confession" referred to by Shirley Stanton concerned her use of narcotics. "I had noticed her pupils and the fact that she didn't drink before," he said. "Drug addicts almost never use liquor. Whoever wanted to silence her apparently knew about her use of morphine."

He explained that if Shirley Stanton was already partly under the influence of the drug, an additional—and fatal—dose could easily have been given her in strong coffee which would disguise the bitterness to her numbed palate.

Holton said, "But this murderer of Miss Stanton whom you have conjured up would have to have a supply of the drug?"

"Probably," McGann agreed. "Or at least know all about her using it and know where she hid it."

"And you have an idea who this person is?"

McGann crushed out his cigarette, pushed back his chair "I have an idea," he said, "but as a lawyer you know how little that means in a court of law or even in front of a desk sergeant. I've got to wait, watch and be ready to move."

Holton did not get up. He seemed paler, more fragile in the immense black leather chair. "You don't care to put your suspicions in more concrete form?"

"Not yet. You can help me though." He added that he would like to go over the Tompkins house at his leisure. "Tell Pearson to give me the run of the place."

The lawyer was shaking his head. "I can't do that. The butler and his wife aren't living there any more. Mr. Tompkins left

them a few thousands so they resigned and moved to Jamaica."
He bent forward and opened a drawer of his desk. "But I can do
better. Here, do what you want up there. The electricity is still
on." The key slid across the blotter and clinked onto the glass-
top desk.

McGann slipped it into his vest pocket. "Fine. You'll hear
from me later. By the way, bet it was nice up in Westchester yesterday."

The black eyes never wavered. "Don't hesitate to ask me anything directly, Mr. McGann. I didn't drive to Westchester. I drove
to Somerville, New Jersey, to my farm. That is beyond Union."

"You should have stopped in Ma Handy's. Hooker Hunyak in
action is interesting in a grim sort of way."

The thin hands fluttered. "I never view violence if I can avoid
it. I hope you will soon clear up this messy business and let us
return to the even tenor of our way."

"I hope so, too," McGann said. He went out and the secretary
smiled at him. The exotic-looking receptionist smiled. McGann
paused at her desk. "Somebody in this office likes pretty girls."

"Holton, Bolton, Durstine and Schwab all like pretty girls,"
the receptionist said. "We like Holton, Bolton and Durstine."

"What's the matter with Schwab?"

She dropped her voice confidentially. "Miss Schwab is not
our type."

"Someday," McGann said, "I'll know enough to stop asking
questions."

Wexton was waiting in the office when he got back. "Why
the hell don't you stay put for five minutes?" he complained.
"Here I am, Secret Agent X-9, with white-hot news and nobody
to report to."

"I'd tell you to keep your shirt on," McGann said, "but I see
you've already done that from yesterday. What is this sizzling
revelation?"

Wexton flopped down in a chair across from McGann's desk. He said importantly, "I have traced the man and woman who followed Ronnie Tompkins from pub to club. I know all about them."

"Who are they?"

"The guy is Peter J. Wilkins and he is a lawyer from Toledo, Ohio. The dame is Mona Coltri, his secretary. They went from Cafe Society Uptown to Cafe Society Downtown, got into a fight with a waiter and wound up at the Charles Street station."

"Obviously a desperate pair. They then—"

"Gave the waiter ten bucks to drop a charge of disorderly conduct and caught the next train back to Toledo Friday morning."

McGann tapped a pencil against his teeth. "That would put them somewhere west of Albany at the time Tompkins was killed. An extraordinary shot."

"I don't think he could have done it with a super-duper snooperscope."

McGann tossed the pencil onto the desk. "That's that," he said. "I never thought much of it anyway."

"Now he tells me," Wexton mourned.

McGann reminded the reporter that he was gaining invaluable experience, a know-how which would undoubtedly pay big dividends in the future. Furthermore, he had a new assignment for him. Wexton could check up to see how many persons in Tompkins' crowd had been on the stuff. He added, "You don't think Ronnie ever danced in the snow, do you?"

"Naw," Wexton said. "He liked a drink but that's as far as it went. I never knew him to take anything stronger. Why?"

"I don't know. That night I went up there, as I told you, I drank alone. And there was something strange about our whole talk, as if he were hypnotized—too calm and smooth if you know what I mean."

"Yes, I don't know what you mean."

"It doesn't matter. Just find out what you can. Find out if Shirley Stanton used morphine before she met Tompkins." He told Wexton about the results of the autopsy. "I have a feeling," he said, "that the Hooker is going to hold me personally responsible for her death."

Wexton clucked. "That's bad. Boy, he's a tough hombre. He's got notches in his notches."

McGann agreed solemnly that El Hunyak made very strong medicine. "You want to be damned sure to roll with the punches if he ever hits you," he said. "Preferably downstairs."

"Let's think of something pleasant—like drinking lunch."

It was beginning to drizzle as they went out, a gray haze dropping down to obscure the tops of the taller buildings. They ate at Rogerson's over on Second Avenue, a sandhog's blue-plate of corned beef and boiled potatoes washed down with draught beer. McGann told Wexton about the coffee cup and the jars now at the chemist's.

The reporter said, "Then you think somebody she knew well enough to sit down with and have a cup of coffee slipped in the overdose?"

"Somebody she knew well enough to let in, anyway. I don't know for sure what was in the cups—yet. But that's about the only way the bitterness of the morphine could have been disguised."

"If Stanton knew who killed Ronnie maybe somebody else does, too. I mean besides the guy who did it."

"Why do you say 'guy'? Why not girl?" Automatically, McGann thought of the moment when he had met Chary Jones in the darkness of the Plaza and she had asked, "*Have they caught her?*" "You people seem damned sure of your murdering sexes."

Wexton lifted his thin shoulders, let them drop. "Just a figure of speech or something. I mean no deduction goes with it."

"That's good." McGann was finishing with a cup of coffee and he stirred it meditatively. "You know having two parts of this investigation in different states isn't going to do it any good from the point of view of the regular authorities."

"You mean that hating each other's guts they won't clear?"

That was what he meant, McGann said. The traditional rivalry between Federal and state men was no greater than that amongst the states and municipalities themselves. New Jersey authorities, investigating the death of Shirley Stanton, would tell New York no more than was absolutely necessary, except in the case of making an arrest. New York would return the compliment.

Eight-state alarms are all very well when you are looking for a couple of automobile thieves but something else when a front-page murder is on tap. The question is whose names are going to read from north to south when the killer is caught?

"Which gives Mrs. McGann's favorite son a chance. My far-flung organization crosses state lines at will."

"Just so long as it doesn't cross them for those awful loose purposes," Wexton said. "I know you Hoover hounds. You're so finicky you'd pinch yourself."

McGann signaled for the check. "That's enough personalities. I've got work to do and so have you. Call me as soon as you have something."

Wexton clapped on the discouraged hat. "Sure, sure. So you can throw it out. Never thought much of it anyway, he says."

"That's the wrong attitude," McGann chided. He leveled an authoritative finger. "No matter what you read, murders are seldom solved by sniffing orchids or by studying the moves in a game of parcheesi. Dogged, yes, dogged detective work is what pays off my boy and you have the perfect mentality for it."

"Woof," Wexton said.

16
AND SOMETHING BLUE

An early fall dusk, made deeper by the drizzling rain, shrouded Manhattan as McGann turned in at the apartment building. His gaze skipped down the row of bells and tiny jewels slid from his hat brim. One spattered on the forefinger pressing the button opposite K. ROGERS.

McGann wiped it on his coat and felt the notebook in the inner pocket. The last entry on its pages was a report from the chemist. The jar with the scratched top had contained coffee, period. That meant nothing had been added to the pot itself.

The ring in the cup also had failed to produce anything extra. But the second jar, with the sample from the other cup, had shown a strong trace of morphine. Assuming that Shirley Stanton had been deliberately poisoned, the murderer had slipped the lethal dose directly into her cup.

Seconds ticked by. If Kathie with the light blue hair answered, McGann could begin to feel that he was chalking up something in the way of progress.

He pressed the button again and leaped for the clicking door on his right.

The foyer bell had said 2D. McGann elected to skip the automatic elevator and risk the exertion. When he reached the second

floor landing he looked about but no door had opened in welcome. He walked along slowly, found 2C, 2B, and retraced his
steps. The door to the apartment of ex-Mrs. Ronnie Tompkins
No. 5 was closed.

McGann knocked. After a moment a voice close against the
panel said, "Who?"

The detective put his face close to the door. "Mack McGann,"
he said. "I met you Saturday night. I'd like to talk to you."

Silence followed, apparently while this information was considered. A dog yelped in an apartment down the hall. Then the
lock of 2D turned and the door slowly opened a few inches. A
chain stopped it. McGann shoved back his hat so that the hall
light could hit his face and waited patiently for the painstaking
perusal.

The door closed again and he heard the chain being slipped
back. Then it swung wide and Kathleen Rogers retreated rigidly
in the dim light, her arms stiffly at her sides, fists clenched.

McGann advanced slowly. She was ghostlike in a dead-white
hostess gown. When she stopped in the center of the living room,
still facing him, he saw that she was owlish in blue-rimmed glasses the exact color of the locks which clustered about her head.

Her voice trembled. "I heard about it. On the radio. I have
let no one else in all day."

He said, "You mean Shirley Stanton?" Then, "Who else tried
to see you?"

The shoulders moved under the white gown. "I couldn't be
sure. That's why I wouldn't open the door. When I asked who
was there, they wouldn't answer."

McGann tried an encouraging smile. "Maybe it was the Fuller
Brush man," he said. "Their first rule is never to identify themselves through closed doors."

It seemed to relax her a trifle. She gestured toward a wide
window-sill above a recessed radiator. "Why don't you put your

hat there? It will dry a bit." She didn't mention his coat. He put the hat at the spot indicated and sat down after she poised on the edge of a chair, hands clasped tightly in her lap.

"What . . . what was it you wanted to talk about?"

"You," McGann said. "But now I see it really isn't necessary."

"How do you mean?"

"I wanted to warn you of your danger but you seem fully aware of it." He smiled reassuringly. "I don't mean that there's anything of extra special concern. Only, living here you were in position to see something important—something which some- one might not want repeated."

Light glinted from the glasses turned toward him. The full orange mouth turned down at the corners. "I'm sorry for the way I spoke to you the other night," Kathleen Rogers said. "You . . . you took me by surprise."

"You did the same to Shirley Stanton."

"Oh . . . that was wicked of me. I know it now. But actually seeing her made something explode inside me. She . . ."

"You disliked her more than you did the others?"

"She stole Ronnie from me. No—don't smile. I really loved him for himself alone and I knew him better than any of 'the others' as you say. Regardless of his eccentricities, Ronnie was social and appreciated his own class more than people might have thought."

She leaned forward as if eager to convince him. "He married showgirls and waitresses as gestures of defiance—he had those emotionally immature impulses—but when he married me, it was as if he had come home at long last. I know that we would have been happy together forever, if only . . ."

"I saw you at the fight camp yesterday," McGann said.

Her pale hand stopped in mid-air. "Ah." Then, "I realized, after thinking it over, how gauche my accusation of Miss Stan- ton had been. I took the opportunity on a drive to stop by and apologize."

"How did she receive it?"

Kathleen Rogers shook her head. "I didn't see her . . . and I couldn't muster courage to ask further." She sighed. "One always thinks there will be another time."

"Mind telling me who you were with?"

"As a matter of fact, I think I would. He has nothing to do with that unfortunate phase of my life. I wouldn't want him involved."

"He's—umm—social, too?"

"Extremely."

"I see." McGann dug in his coat pocket. "Mind if I smoke?"

"Please do. No—no, thanks. I'll have one of my own." She moved gracefully to the mantle and fitted a thin cigarette into a blue holder.

McGann indicated the holder and the matching glasses. "You were a symphony in red the other night. That's an attractive touch."

"Thank you. When I found that I really would have to wear glasses I thought I might do something with them."

"Those look like special cigarettes."

She held out the box. "Do try them. They're Arabian. I can't abide domestic tobaccos."

McGann accepted and lit both with a flourish. He inhaled deeply. When he stopped coughing, he wiped his eyes. "Among Arabs who know tobacco best," he said, "it's Old Muezzins two to one. What's in these—pulverized prayer-rugs?"

It was the first time that he had ever seen her smile. The big eyes softened. "You have to get used to them. I really should have warned you. Perhaps if I mix you a drink—"

He eyed her narrowly. "Some rare Tibetan cocktail? The stuff that makes yaks jump over the Himalayas?"

She was opening a liquor cabinet. "Nothing farther than Scotland." A pinch bottle glowed warmly. "All right?"

"Against the weather," McGann said.

They sipped and faced each other in silence for a moment. "Anything you want to say will be in confidence," McGann promised. "You understand my connection is unofficial."

"Really, Mr. McGann, I have no information."

"People often have it without being aware of it. Suppose I ask some questions? It may save other lives—even yours."

"Very well."

"Earlier today I talked with a real estate broker. I learned that originally you were offered a front apartment. But you selected this one. Why?"

Her shoulders moved back. "All right," she said defiantly. "It was small of me, and mean. I admit it. I took it to annoy them."

"Ronnie and any subsequent wives?"

"Yes. Oh, I knew that they would start out laughing at me over there. I knew they would look at that horrible portrait of me and the paintings of the others and laugh."

"Is that what happened when you were married to him?"

She rose and began to pace agitatedly. "Isn't it a shameful thing to admit? But I did it, too. Somehow Ronnie made you do it. He seemed to be so much in love with you and so contemptuous of those who had gone before. You felt certain that you were the one who would hold him forever."

McGann said relentlessly, "Which in your case was about five weeks."

"Six." Her fingers curled over the back of a chair, the nails pressed into the upholstery. "When he told me to get out, I couldn't believe it. I simply couldn't believe it." Her voice stung. "I could have killed him, he was so cold about it. I'm not afraid to say it, Mr. McGann, I could have killed him then without a single pang of conscience."

"But someone else beat you to it?"

She resumed the restless pacing. "I'm sure I would never have done anything. It was just one of those wild ideas—a woman scorned and that sort of thing. I was getting over it. Really I was."

McGann had pinched out the Arabian cigarette. He palmed it and lit one of his own. "I was looking over some old clippings the other night," he said. "There was an *American Weekly* story about your hunting trip to Africa. It said you were a wonderful shot."

To his surprise, she gave a short laugh. "You're wasting your time, Mr. McGann. As a matter of fact, I missed an elephant at thirty yards."

The detective grinned and stood up. "I know. Now would you show me your observation tower?"

The white figure moved ahead of him. Kathleen Rogers had wide shoulders and a splendid carriage. "No, don't turn on the light," McGann said. "I want to see outside, too."

He moved warily through the gloom of the bedroom, the windows of which opened directly onto the court across from the Tompkins' study. She pulled the cord opening the venetian blinds and they stood close together at the window.

Thin rain was still slanting down. You could see it if you looked at the naked electric bulb above the service entrance of the next apartment.

As his eyes became accustomed to the darkness, McGann could make out the iron tracery of the fire escape opposite and the dark window of the study which had been replaced since Spanish's spectacular exit. "Could I borrow your opera glasses?" he asked.

She hesitated. "I guess it's no use pretending I don't have any, is it?"

"Not really," McGann said.

She opened the nearest drawer of the vanity and handed him a pair. They were small but well made, and powerful, he soon discovered. He followed the spidery fire-escape to the top, skipped across the dark windows, and paused to watch a girl in a light blue bra who was brushing her hair in the apartment. When she finished brushing, she adjusted a shoulder strap, then walked over and pulled the shade down.

"Sabotage," McGann said.

"What's that?"

"The investigation is up against a drawn shade—I mean a stone wall. How long has Tompkins' place been like this?"

"There hasn't been a soul over there since early yesterday."

McGann lowered the glasses and turned to face her in the gloom. "What really happened over there Friday night? I looked out once and saw a light go out. I'm quite sure it was in this apartment."

For a long breath, she stood gazing at the rain. "That's just it," she said. "I didn't actually see anything. Here's how it was."

She walked across the room and turned on the light in the adjoining bath. Enough escaped through the half-open door partially to illuminate the bedroom.

"I was creaming my face in the bathroom," she said, "when I heard a sharp noise like a shot or a firecracker from across the court. I walked in here where it was dark and looked over."

"Fine," McGann said. "What did you see?"

"Well, like I say—nothing really. The window of Ronnie's study was open and the shade was up. I could see a light in the room and the firelight but that was all."

"Wait a minute," McGann said. "You must have seen more than that. Did you come right in here the instant you heard the noise or did you wait for a while and then decide to look?"

"I came in right away. If I'm going to admit I'm a snoop, I might as well be a good one."

McGann moved briskly to the lighted room. He swung around and stepped back to the bedroom windows. "That only takes about two seconds, elapsed time," he mused aloud. "It would hardly give a person time to get the study window open, let alone go up or down the fire escape. You're absolutely certain you came right in and looked?"

"Face full of cream and all."

McGann shook his head as if to clear it. He seemed finally to accept it. "Since there wasn't time to raise the window and get away from it between the sound of the shot and when you looked out, it must have been open before the shot."

"I suppose so."

"How was the sound, quite clear? I think you said sharp?"

"Very distinct. My own window was down a few inches from the top."

"All right. So you looked out and things were as you described. Then what?"

"I watched for a few minutes and heard a crash over there."

"That was me playing Superman with the door."

"I realized that this room was half-lighted and someone might see me, so I went back and switched off the bathroom light and came over again to watch."

"That was the light I saw go out."

"You were looking out the window when I returned. I stayed here for hours, absolutely petrified. I heard the sirens and saw police come in." She gestured toward a small ivory cabinet on the night-table. "Somehow I knew what had happened. When it came over the radio it was no great surprise."

Lost in thought, both stared at the building across the court. Both seemed to see it at the same instant. A match flared up in the dark of the Tompkins' study. The tiny tongue of yellow flame moved slowly across the room, then hovered uncertainly for a moment.

McGann had the glasses on it. "Snap off that light," he said. In a moment the room was plunged into darkness. He could see a shadowy figure and the match went out.

The hostess gown rustled and she was close beside him. Her breath was warm on his cheek. "What is it?" she whispered. A second match flared in Tompkins' study, and moved steadily toward the art gallery door and out of sight.

"That's damned funny," McGann said. "The servants are gone and even if they came back the electricity's still on. Holton told me. I'm going over."

Kathleen Rogers' hand sought his and pressed. "For heaven's sake, be careful," she pleaded. "My God, if there should be any more. I—"

"Can I get through the basement to the back? Then I wouldn't have to go around the block."

"Yes, of course. That is, I think so. The elevator runs to the basement. There should be a rear door."

McGann heard the chain slide back into place as the automatic elevator hummed to a stop. He stepped in, punched B and held his finger on it. It let him out in a dim and musty corridor. He found a narrow hall leading back, opened a door and went up several steps to the courtyard between the buildings.

He glanced back and up and thought he could see the white gown motionless behind the open blind. His gaze darted to the dark study window and then he ran quickly across to the service entrance, through which he and Frazier Farwell once had made their way to the street. Was that only Friday night? It seemed much longer ago. The rain on his hair and face reminded him that he had left his hat on the radiator in Kathleen Rogers' apartment.

He plunged through the narrow hall of the building and found himself beside the brownstone steps leading up to the Tompkins' home. The front was as dark as the rear. A car went by, heading toward the park, its tires whining in the slick, and across the street a couple hurried along, their heads down against the drizzle.

Noiselessly, McGann crept up the brownstone steps. His hand tried the knob on the front door. It was locked. Probing fingers found the key which Holton had given him that morning in a vest pocket. He slid it soundlessly into the lock, cursed softly when it turned with a sharp click. The door melted beneath his touch.

In the foyer, he stopped, listening. To his right, he knew now, was Tompkins' art gallery of ex-wives. One door was on this hall. It must be closed because he could see nothing but there came to his nostrils the unmistakable odor of newly-struck matches. Whoever was there was afraid to turn on the lights.

Just to the left inside that door, he remembered a wall switch. He had already started forward when he heard a ripping, tearing sound within. McGann slid out of his raincoat and let it drop to the floor. He thought, I hope I live to regret this, and swung open the art gallery door, his free hand groping for the switch.

17

THE HOOK

Lights sprang from the seven portraits and from the wall brackets run in for the cocktail wake. Hooker Hunyak stood across the room before the half-demolished frame holding the painting of Shirley Stanton.

In one of his powerful hands a match glowed weakly. The other dropped from the partly pulled-out canvas.

"Hello," McGann said. He heard the door click shut behind him. All other evidences of the party had been removed. There was nothing in the room but the portraits, Hooker Hunyak and himself.

The match burned close to Hunyak's fingers and he flicked it to the rug without taking his gaze from the detective. His eyes were wide and calm, almost kind. He said, "Ya dirty, lousy sonabitch."

McGann nodded toward the portrait. "I don't blame you for wanting it," he said. "It's a beautiful thing. If it disappears, I won't know about it and the Metropolitan will never care."

Hunyak moved lithely, noiselessly toward him. Almost automatically, it seemed, he had risen to the balls of his feet. The lighting, the quiet like that immediately after an opening bell gave McGann the weird feeling that he was in the ring at Madison Square Garden.

He moved slowly, casually backward. There was room for only a few steps. Hunyak stopped, poised, two arm lengths away. His lethal fists were brown clubs at his sides. He said, "I told ya nothing had better happen to her. Now I'm gonna do what I shoulda done then."

McGann raised a hand protestingly as the heavy fists came up. "Wait a minute. Doesn't somebody have to sing the Star-Spangled Banner or something? Let's—"

Hunyak's left flashed out and McGann used one of the few precious steps back to take it high on the left chest. It stung and whirled him partly around so that he was coming forward when the fighter's piston right thudded into the V below his ribs with the snap and power of a mallet on a stake.

McGann felt the air rush out his nose and mouth, felt himself jerk with the sucking reflex of collapsed lungs clawing breath. He flung his arms around Hunyak, clinching desperately for a moment's respite.

In that brief instant, faces close, he looked into the curiously gentle eyes with a thrill of knowledge. They were frozen in that spurious innocence, unseeing except for the kill. It was as if someone had pulled a switch on the human part of Hooker Hunyak, leaving only the trained fighting machine that could not stop until the object it had been sent against was broken and bleeding.

McGann's chest swelled gratefully with the close air of the room. It was possible to hold the clinch for a few seconds only. Hunyak brought his fists up, close together, close against his own body in the traditional break and forced his elbows up and out. It threw McGann back. The fighter followed through with a brisk shove and danced forward, ready to strike through the first opening.

McGann thought, This is murder, but personally. To fight a man of 190 to 200 pounds, in good condition, was dangerous and difficult even if you yourself had a lot to offer. To be faced by a professional heavyweight, a leading contender, was like being led to the slaughter. You were a duffer playing Bobby Jones, a sand-lot pitcher facing Ruth.

He shifted to Hunyak's right, away from the explosive left hook and shot a jab to the fighter's mouth. Hunyak's lips twitched in a mirthless grin. He crouched, shoulder high, bounced up on spring-steel legs and drove a powerhouse left to McGann's heart. McGann felt his knees buckle, the rug came up and clapped him on the back; rearing far above him was an even more gigantic Hooker.

Mechanically, McGann rolled away to forestall the leather but Hunyak waited patiently. He didn't exactly retire to a neutral corner but McGann was pleasantly surprised to see that years of ring training seemed to make him react spontaneously. McGann scrambled to his feet and now he had most of the room behind him for a fighting retreat.

He was breathing hard. The gallery seemed filled with the pounding of his heart. Even as he tried to plan some better defensive campaign, Hunyak was on him. McGann knew what was going to happen the instant that the routine started. The picture of a huge chocolate body collapsing in the sparring ring flashed before him as Hunyak tapped him on the chest with a left. The right to the midsection was a split-second behind and McGann threw himself violently to the side away from the left hook that he knew was next.

He almost made it. The bruising knuckles burned his cheek below the right eye, snapping his head smartly back and he sprawled ignominiously again on the rug while lights danced briskly. The seven beautiful loves of Ronnie Tompkins gazed serenely down upon him.

Hooker Hunyak gazed down upon him with equal calm—a killer thoroughly conversant with his work. The club-like knuckles were moving in tight little circles, waiting for him to rise again. The left foot was out, almost against his own perpendicular soles.

McGann had been in a daze comprised of equal parts of surprise and disbelief. Somehow he had been hoping that Hunyak would come out of it, drop it. Now intense anger swelled within him. This big bastard wasn't going to stop until McGann was a bleeding wreck. Well, he wasn't standing up again under the same circumstances.

Where the hell were the rules if a professional with a twenty-five-pound advantage didn't see anything wrong with the match? McGann hooked his right foot behind Hunyak's heel. He jammed the instep of his left foot just below the fighter's knee. With perfect timing and all of his strength, he pulled on the first and pushed with the second.

Hunyak tilted back. His free leg left the carpet and for a tremendous second he hung in the air in a slow back-flip. He threshed about wildly with his big hands and then he came down full length with a crash calculated to start the back teeth from their sockets.

McGann whipped forward with the crash, flung himself upon the breathless fighter. His left hand closed on Hunyak's right wrist, his right arm went under and back and he strained on the double wrist-lock.

Hunyak's elbow cracked ominously and his face contorted in pain. McGann was seized with a wild impulse to break it for him. The fighter's scream cut through the red fog that seemed to fill the room, and McGann let go. He swung his flat hand in a flashing arc as Hunyak's head came up. The edge caught the fighter just below the base of the nose where the nerves are concentrated and Hunyak went limp.

Breathing hard, McGann slid back a few feet and rested, waiting for Hunyak to come to. He was reasonably certain that the fight was over. It was a long time since he had used judo.

You had to be careful when you played it for keeps, particularly that blow below the nose, or you'd have another corpse on your hands. That, of course, was infinitely superior to being a corpse on somebody else's hands.

He had lighted a cigarette and was puffing quietly when Hooker Hunyak stirred and groaned. The fighter started to sit up, grimaced in pain when he put weight on his right arm. He struggled to a sitting position and the eyes he turned on McGann were filled with wondering resentment as well as suddenly returned sanity.

"Ya fight with yuh feet," he complained.

McGann let the cigarette dangle from his lip and touched the tender spot below his eye where Hunyak's hook had burned past. "I operate under the rules of the Marquis of Florsheim," he said. "This proves conclusively that a prizefighter cannot defeat a gorilla in open combat."

Hunyak was feeling his upper lip and looking for blood. "I don't know whatcha talking about," he said, "but ya got somethin' there, pal. Ya got somethin'." He flexed his arm cautiously.

"It ain't busted," he announced finally.

"Gloryosky," McGann said, "that makes me feel glad all over." He got to his feet and shook himself into his clothes which were considerably screwed around. Hooker Hunyak also got to his feet and the two surveyed the room.

"I was just takin' her pitcher," the fighter said apologetically. "She didn't like it here—she said so, and—" he looked sheepish, "—I wanted it."

"I know," McGann said. "I tried to tell you before to help yourself but you tuned out on me."

"Ya mean it's all right. Ya ain't sore?"

McGann shrugged. "Go ahead. I ain't—I'm not the watchman here. I just saw someone striking matches and wanted to know what gave."

"I didn't wanta try turning on no lights," Hunyak explained. In answer to McGann's question, he produced a key similar to the one the detective had received from Amos Holton. "I knew where Shirley kept it," he said. "She had it long's I knew her, anyways."

This is wonderful, McGann thought. If Ronnie Tompkins had handed out keys, and not bothered to change locks as often as he did wives—then everybody and her brother had had access to the place. He kept the key, putting it with Holton's. Then he helped Hunyak take the canvas of Shirley Stanton from the frame. For a minute he contemplated the painting of Charity Jones, admiring the flawless features and faint smile.

"Ya know," McGann said, "ya got somethin' there, pal." He conquered the impulse. "I guess I'd better not. Not yet, anyway. Two in one night would be too much. Somebody might get suspicious."

Hunyak's thanks was warm. He seemed a different man. He said, "You're okay, mister. Any time ya want me tuh take care of someone—" He paused, remembering. "Hell, I guess ya don't need much help."

"You can help me in another way," McGann said. He got his raincoat from the front hall and retrieved the notebook. "Just start by telling me where you were Friday afternoon."

Hunyak said he had been at Stillman's gym watching the champion work out for pointers. Was he with anyone? Well, not exactly. Shirley Stanton had dropped him off and gone on to buy some junk. What time did she come back for him? He wasn't sure but it must have been late. He was hungry. That was his clock.

Did he talk to anyone? Sure, sure. Some of the guys. Moe, Joe. Who knew anybody's last name? How did Shirley act when she came back? Well, kinda funny, jittery like. Snapped because she caught him swipin' a couple puffs of a cigar. Ain't tha't a laugh? With the gym fulla smoke anyway.

The flattened face twitched in sudden grief. "Alla same, she was a swell dame," Hunyak said. "She was sure swell to me." He pounded his big fist slowly into his open palm. "Don't know what I'm gonna do now. Maybe Ma Handy'll manage me."

McGann shoved the notebook into his jacket pocket. He clapped Hunyak gently on the shoulder. "You'll do all right," he said. "Now you'd better beat it with that picture before I notice it's gone."

He walked as far as the stoop with the fighter, who appeared to be without hat or topcoat. Rain still slanted down. Hunyak slipped the rolled-up canvas inside his suit coat. "I'll grab a hack," he said. "Be seeing ya, pal."

"So long, pal," McGann said.

He turned back into the foyer, closed the door and switched on the light. The grandfather clock had stopped at 10:43 but what day or night McGann did not know. He stood immobile.

The shadowed love nest of Ronnie Tompkins was heavy with silence and the first faint trace of the mustiness which would move in now. It would come slowly at first, then thick and cloying, smothering remembrance of the laughing lips the house had known and the weeping eyes.

McGann moved forward, the carpet whispering beneath his feet as he headed for the study.

18
MYSTERY MANSION

McGann pushed open the study door and felt around for an electric switch. Yellow light from an overhead dome washed over the big desk, the leather chair behind it. He pulled the shades down and wondered if Kathleen Rogers were still across the courtyard and was observing the lightened squares.

His gaze circled the room slowly, came to rest on the small throw rug in the center. He lifted a corner of it with his toe and studied the irregular stain before kicking it back. He tried to recapture the mental picture he first had gained of the study—warm and rich and gave it up. It was still and remote, cold like anything that had been dead for three days.

His watch said 6:24—almost the hour that they had heard the shot. Pure coincidence, of course. McGann took a deep breath, then rubbed the spot on his diaphragm where Hunyak had made like a mule. He moved carefully to the desk, noticed that the record-player had been pushed to the wall near it, and sat down.

Ronnie Tompkins had done well by himself. The desk was massive, expensive. Now it was littered with papers where police had gone through it and the bare spots had a thin covering of dust. McGann drew an X in the dust with his forefinger and wiped it on the blotter. He pulled open the center drawer and looked at a hodge-podge of papers, pencils and pens, a letter opener. Some of the papers appeared to be monthly statements of various companies; there was an advertisement from the manufacturers of an abdominal belt—"Lose Twenty Pounds in Five Minutes; Look and Feel Years Younger."

O'Callahan would almost surely have taken anything that was of obvious importance or might have some bearing on the murder. Later, Holton or an assistant would collect every scrap to be filed or destroyed.

Thinking of Holton made McGann swing around and lift the cover of the radio-phonograph. There was no record on the brown-felt turntable. He drew a similar blank in the cabinet. The wall safe stood open and empty behind a drape. Holton must have taken the record of Tompkins' will with him.

McGann pulled open the right-hand drawer of the desk. That was where Tompkins had kept the gun and the cartridges. He wondered if the gun had been there on the night of the murder or whether the killer had obtained it earlier and brought it back. Wexton had said that police were unable to account for one cartridge. Where the hell had it got to and why?

The phone was on the desk and without bothering about fingerprints any more McGann picked it up. The dial tone came on and he dialed the Waldorf and asked for Chary's room.

She said "Hello" in a small, cautious voice.

"That's a very trite way to start a conversation," McGann said. "It's been worked to death. But from you it sounds wonderful. How are you doing?"

"Oh," Chary said, her tone sharpening. "Well, it's about time. Really, Mac, I expected to hear from you a little more often. I mean, how long—"

"Whoa," McGann said. "When I called this morning you were that happy child. How come?"

There was a moment's silence. Her voice was friendlier. "All right, I'm sorry. But it is getting on to dinner time and this bird in a gilded cage routine *can* be overdone and I'm young—"

"And beautiful."

". . . and hungry and how about it?"

McGann was sorry, he was desolate. There was nothing in the wide world that he would rather do than eat—providing that he could at the same time feast his eyes upon Miss Charity Jones. But duty was a stern master. He was at work. He said, "Call room service."

"You mean I can't even go down to Peacock Alley?"

"No." The pause was frigid. "Look," McGann said, assuming a gay air. "Tell you what we'll do. You eat in your room and I'll come by and pick you up about ten o'clock and we'll go out."

"Dancing?"

"Definitely. The mad mazurka. I'll bring my castanets."

"Wonderful!" Her laugh was warm, relieved. "I'll wait for you," she said, "until five seconds after ten." She hung up.

"Hmm," McGann said. He replaced the instrument in its cradle with great delicacy, and noticed the calendar pad on the desk. It read Saturday, Oct. 11. Tompkins had been slain on Friday. Who had torn off the page? he wondered.

Something had been written on the Friday page, he decided. A sharp pencil had left a few faint indentations. He tried to make them out in the overhead light, decided he couldn't and took it over to the lamp under which he had sat for that first interview.

The strong bulb was still in it. Holding the pad at a slant, he could see scattered letters. There was a Chelsea number which faded out and a rather plain . . . ton. Holton? His eye quickened. Halfway down the page was an unmistakable Mc and after it the letters . . . nda . . . Sunday? Monday? But he had been called on Friday. What had caused the change in plans, brought him to the strange mansion earlier? Could it have been Frazier Farwell's babbling?

McGann tore off the page and put it into his pocket. He leafed through the remainder of the year. For the rest of October there were cryptic entries, "Lunch G.," "Birthday S.," then snowy blanks.

He put the pad back on the desk and continued his prowl of the room. The fireplace was hugely cheerless now, a black cavern with a floor of ashes and a few charred bits of logs. He poked among them with a pencil but there was no piece of calendar pad or anything else that he could see.

For a moment he stood looking from the desk to the fireplace and then to the throw rug. The silence of the great old house was like a smothering blanket. To break it, he cleared his throat and lit a cigarette.

Apparently satisfied that there was nothing else in the room, he turned his attention to the doors leading out of it. There were three; one into the art gallery, one into the long hall and one in the far corner near the window. Had the killer stepped into the art gallery at the very moment that the second door was being broken down? If Kathleen Rogers had been telling the truth, no one could have gone down the fire-escape between the noise of the explosion and the time she got to her observation post.

McGann tried the door near the window. It opened onto a little platform and an overhead chain threw sickly beams when he pulled it. It was a servant's stairway, spiraling up and down, and it was close and warm. He descended, striking matches after the turn, and coming out in an old-fashioned kitchen where hanging pans threw back the tiny light of the match.

This, then, was where the Pearsons rested between bird-walks. The butler and his wife would have had easy access to the study if they had returned early from Croton-on-Hudson, or, in fact, if they never had gone there at all. He made a mental note to check the Hudson division timetable.

Turning, McGann ascended the creaking spiral. A door opened into the second-floor hall. The top floor had a transverse corridor with doors opening into a storage room, into the rear suite where he had found Farwell and into the hall. Visitors would never have been able to surprise Mrs. Pearson on the front stairway with an armful of soiled linen.

McGann went back to the second floor and along it to the front bedroom which he guessed had been Tompkins'. He was certain of it when he switched on the light. The only decoration was on the dresser. It was a fine portrait of a placid woman dressed in the fashion of thirty years before, and the inscription said, "Love, Mother."

McGann thought, That was Tompkins' underlying trouble, of course. Always trying, figuratively, to marry his own mother. Always being disappointed in anything less than a false perfection. He smiled. Freud, Jung, and Adler would have been proud of him for this deduction. Even Mary Haworth would not have been displeased.

He opened and shut drawers of the dresser, riffling through them expertly. Beautiful military brushes of mahogany and silver, socks, ties, shirts, underwear. In the closet were rows of shoes, all correctly aligned and held stiff by shoe-trees. Rows of suits, browns, blues, plaids, grays. Tails and two dinner jackets. He took out the dinner jackets and looked at them but neither had been salvaged from the body—there was no .32 mark with its rough brown splotch on the back. That one probably had been ordered burned by Holton and was already cleaned, mended and on sale somewhere.

The bathroom showed none of Ronnie Tompkins' apparent love of luxury. It was plain, even old-fashioned with a tub mounted on claw feet and a circular shower with a white curtain.

McGann opened the medicine chest. Bottles of liniment, iodine, aspirin, hair tonic, hair tint. McGann picked out the latter. "Fountain of youth," he said. So Tompkins had cheated a little. He put it back. A nail scissors and file, undoubtedly for emergency jobs only. Ronnie would never have passed up the chance to hold hands with a manicurist and potential bride.

There was a wicker clothes hamper in the corner. Mrs. Pearson had not bothered to empty it before she had clutched her legacy to her bosom and taken off for Jamaica. Shorts, handkerchiefs, socks, a couple of dress shirts, three business shirts.

There was a dark brown smear on the front of one of the dress shirts and McGann took it out and looked at it, rubbing his finger over it lightly. Blood? It was not the shirt in which Tompkins had met his death, for again there was no bullet hole in the back nor was there even any discoloration there.

Had there been some recent nightclub fight of which he had not been told? Tompkins wore formal attire frequently. Had someone even come to the house and clipped him, necessitating a change of linen? He held the shirt in his hand a long time and stood pondering before dropping it back and closing the hamper.

Thoughtfully, McGann selected a towel from the rack and shined his rain-splattered shoes. Kathleen Rogers had not looked out of her window until she heard the sound of the shot, so the killer could have come into the study from the fire-escape or one of the three doors.

But the murderer could not have left by the fire-escape or she would have seen someone. McGann returned to the bedroom and brushed his hair with the mahogany and silver set. Therefore, the killer probably had been in the house at the very time McGann was examining the study or telephoning police.

With appreciation, McGann selected a deep blue tie with an odd figure from the scores on a wall rack and substituted the striped one he had been wearing. He admired the result in Tompkins' mirror.

So the killer could have slipped out the front door while McGann was gawking out of the window or could even have left by the downstairs servants' entrance. To return as the well-known innocent bystander or interested spectator? He found a clothes brush and removed the lint he had picked up in his brief but spirited encounter with Hooker Hunyak.

At least no one had tried to tell him that Tompkins didn't have an enemy in the world. That was a favorite expression of startled relatives when someone was polished off. They'd swear, "Joe didn't have an enemy in the world" and then you'd find out he'd been feuding with everybody north of Fourteenth Street.

Tompkins had ten million dollars which is ten million motives if you murder cheaply enough. McGann got up close to the mirror and examined the skin burn from the Hooker's hook. It could have been worse. But as far as motives went, money wasn't the only one—plenty of people would have paid for the privilege of canceling Tompkins' contract.

Whoever had killed Tompkins also had killed Shirley Stanton and furthermore had known that the redhead was a morphine addict. There could be no doubt but that she was killed because of what she knew, or at least suspected. McGann decided that he could get by without a second shave and that there wasn't time anyway.

He retraced his steps through the house, turning out all of the lights, and got his raincoat from the foyer. The front door snapped shut when he pulled it behind him. It had stopped raining but the streets still glistened.

He walked around the block to get his hat from the Rogers' apartment. This time there was no answering click when he pressed her bell. He tried it three times, then selected a bell on the top floor at random and pressed that.

When he got inside, a woman was calling down the stairwell, "Yes?"

McGann looked up. "Did you order twenty-two sandwiches from the drugstore?" he asked.

"What?"

"Ten with and twelve without?"

"No," the voice said and a door slammed. McGann walked over and pounded on Kathleen Rogers' door. There was no answer. He listened but it was silent within and the knob would not turn. Great, he thought. Go through life having your hat thrown out of apartments and the one time you want it they won't open the door.

Had she gone out or was she inside, now too frightened to trust the chain? He rapped again and called, "It's McGann, Miss Rogers. McGann. Large M, small c, large G . . ."

"Wassa matter, wassa noise?" A squat Italian had come up from the basement. He glared at McGann belligerently. He had superintendent written all over him.

"I had a hat when I came in," McGann said. "And I'll have a hat when I go out."

The superintendent took a step backward. "We no wanta hats," he said. "No canavassing in building."

McGann walked over slowly. He stared down at the superintendent who seemed undecided between fight and flight. He said darkly, "You haven't heard the last of this, Ravelli. Someone stole one of my mittens once and I worked on the case until I outgrew them anyway. Put that in your hat and smoke it."

The super's contemptuous snort followed him out the door. "Putta smoke in your hat," he said. He seemed surprised at a sudden discovery. "Hey, you no gotta hat!"

McGann stopped in the corner cigar store and got a pack of cigarettes. He took out the notebook and called the Rogers' apartment. There was no answer.

It was 7:35. He looked up the number of Irma Nelson's apartment in the East Seventies, and dialed that. When she came on he told her that he'd like to talk to her for a little while.

"Darling," she said. "We'd love to see you!"

"Who's 'we'?"

"Just me and the goldfish."

"Put their blinders on," McGann said. "I'll be right up."

19

BLONDE AT BAY

Pink, sleek lounging pajamas containing Irma Nelson shimmered ahead of McGann into the living room. A cozy fire lazed on the hearth. In the corner a radio was playing a low waltz. She swung around and smiled, holding out a hand for his coat.

"I hope you don't mind my coming in through the door," McGann said. "I can't get used to windows."

"Always bringing up my past," Irma Nelson said. Her hair was fine gold in the firelight and he noticed that her lipstick matched the pink of the pajamas. She indicated the sofa before the fire. "Deposit the derriere." He looked surprised and she added, "This is a word. I got it from Earl Wilson."

"You went right to the seat of knowledge," McGann admitted. It was warm and relaxing on the sofa. He heard the clink of ice and glass in a moment and the hiss of a siphon.

She handed him a cool drink and curled up opposite him on the sofa. Her eyes crinkled. "All right, grill me, darling," she said. "But be careful, I'm tender."

McGann considered the glass, took a tentative sip. It was Scotch and strong. He took a longer pull. He asked, "How's your tatting coming along?"

"It's not tatting, it's embroidering."

161

"So it's embroidering. Getting much done?"

Her hands were clasped about her knees. "Nope, I'm giving it up. It gets a girl into too much trouble. I never dreamed before that it was dangerous."

"It's not dangerous if you don't lie about it."

The smile froze on her face and the long fingers tightened. "What d'ya mean by a crack like that?"

"I'll be more specific. You told me that you embroidered the name 'Irma' on a doll pillow, and forgot it at Ronnie's the day he was murdered."

She nodded wordlessly.

"At least the last part of that is a lie. You didn't leave it there." He explained about the ruse concerning the tapestry. "You fell for it."

For a long moment their gazes locked. "Now that you mention it," she said, "I *did* lie about that. But it doesn't mean I was the lucky one who got to shoot Ronnie. You can't pin that on me at least."

"No." He put down the empty glass and she got up and took it. Over his shoulder, he said, "But you were right about Kathleen Rogers having the apartment across the court. She saw plenty."

The ice tongs clashed into the tray. When she handed him the glass again her hand was trembling. If she was struggling with an urge to ask "What?" she mastered it. She stood looking into the fire. "Wouldn't you know," she said, "that Ronnie would cause me even more trouble dead than alive." She gave a short laugh. "I gave him the best weeks of my life and what have I got to show for it. Nothing but a fortune and worries."

McGann decided that either he was getting weaker or Scotch was getting stronger. Then he remembered that it had been a long time and a lot had happened since he had eaten. The ice tumbled in the glass when he raised it.

"Shirley Stanton's worries are over."

"God, yes. What an awful thing." The blonde head came around. "It doesn't scare me, though, if that's what you'd like to think."

"I don't like to think—period. It wears out the brain cells." He waved a hand. "Thinking is a thankless thing." He favored the sound of that and said it again. "Sit down," he invited. "No, wait—here, while you're up."

The pink pajamas were a pleasant blaze all their own in the firelight. She stood before him for a minute when she returned so he swung his legs up onto the sofa and she sat beside him. He slid down comfortably and rested his head on the upholstered arm. The glass was cool on his shirt front.

He began to talk, easily and gently. He told her about Shirley Stanton's use of drugs, about Kathleen Rogers' terror, about Hooker Hunyak's devotion. He led her in thought through the old house which she had reason to know so well.

"From what I can gather," McGann said, "Tompkins wasn't a bad sort and he was generous with people he liked. He didn't have any serious quarrels with anyone that we know about. Yet somebody killed him—and incidentally let you get mixed up in it."

She just watched him and he went on. "You people who surrounded Tompkins seem to have had an unofficial club or clique or whatever you want to call it. Some of you hated others, that's true, but you all hung together. Maybe you couldn't keep in touch with Ronnie and his money without putting up with each other. I don't know. You partied at one another's places?"

"Sometimes."

"You've had them all up here? Gladys Mars, that chap Besser, Farwell, Stanton and the rest?"

"Yes."

"How about Dink Wexton, the reporter?"

"He's been here."

"Chary Jones? Holton?"

"Just Holton."

He let the coolness slide down his throat where it immediately turned warm. Irma Nelson was more subdued than he had ever known her. She seemed to be waiting quietly for whatever might be next. He said, "It's unfortunate that Solly got so inquisitive about Tompkins' movements."

A slight movement told how she had tensed. "Frazier Farwell talks too damned much," she said. "He thinks he's always in front of a mike."

"What was Solly after, anyway?"

There was nothing to it, Irma Nelson swore. Absolutely nothing. To begin with, Solly had not been asking about the layout of the Tompkins home. He'd of asked her, wouldn't he? It was true that she hadn't been married to Ronnie long but at least it had been long enough to permit her to look over the house.

"He wanted to know about Ronnie's plans for the south."

"That was a business deal," Irma Nelson said. "Solly wanted to help a couple of the boys interest Ronnie in a proposition."

"And they wanted to talk to him when he was friendly and relaxed under a palm tree, that all?"

"That's all." She took his empty glass and started to rise. "No, really," he said. "I wouldn't want to impose on your hospitality." He swung around her and stood up. "I'll fix it myself. I wouldn't want to be a burden."

But she had risen anyway when he came back and he walked up close, looking down slightly into her eyes. "It was a foolish idea," he said. "Just because you figured you could dream up an alibi for the time of Tompkins' murder, you stuck your neck out about the pillow."

"Why should I do that?"

He made it sharp and quick. "Because you think Solly did it."

Her lashes fell slowly and her head bent. He talked to the part in the golden tresses. "You think he had your trinket along and stopped in Ronnie's and shot him and either dropped it or left it on some wild impulse. You think—"

She had her clenched fists pressed together before her and suddenly she leaned forward and put her face against his neck. Her shoulders were quivering, and her voice sounded in muffled gasps. "My God," she said, "I only want a break . . . just a break. Everyone . . . everytime I think, this is it—something happens. I try to go along . . . try to be a right guy, and some crazy, damn thing . . ."

McGann reached over and put the glass on the mantel and patted her back. The sobs increased and she pressed more closely to him. The shining hair was smooth against his cheek. "Look," he said, "this won't do any good. You've got to get hold of yourself, Miss Nelson—Irma—maybe it will all—"

She moved her face more quietly against him. The warmth of the fire and the drinks blended in him and he held her there gently. He was still holding her when Solly Spanish stood in the room, poised there a full second before the door slammed. His dark eyes shone from narrowed slits. Spanish said, "I'm keeping you up, maybe. I should apologize."

Irma Nelson twisted from McGann's arms and got behind him. Solly Spanish came slowly around the far end of the sofa. His hand fluttered toward his shoulder, then he seemed to remember and it dropped.

The dark eyes went over McGann. "That permit of yours doesn't say that it's all right to fool around with other guys' wives, does it?"

McGann looked around at the girl. She was rigid with her hands behind her. He got out of the way and she gasped as Spanish started forward.

McGann retrieved his drink from the mantel. "Stop it, kids," he said, "you're killing me. It's a wonderful performance but the plot's too familiar." He took a drink. "The badger game went out with gas lights and corset covers."

Spanish tried gamely to carry the bluff. "It's a hell of a thing for a man to come home to, right? You're a cop. Why don't you go out and throw your arms around a burglar?"

"Why don't you close doors and just walk in instead of arriving like a rocket-ship?" McGann countered. "You give yourself away. Natural does it." He looked at Irma. "And when you cry your heart out be sure that your mascara runs. Your eyes are drier than a millionaire's baby."

"Just the same—" Spanish sputtered.

"Oh, shut up, Solly," Irma said. "It didn't work, so forget it." She grinned at McGann and patted his cheek. "My little sharpie," she said. "Let me fix you a fresh one."

"No, thanks," McGann said. "I've really got to run." He held out a hand. "I know I was supposed to dash out in confusion but I need the property, please."

She shrugged and brought her other hand from behind her and gave him his notebook. "Thanks," he said, and sighed. "It wasn't my personality after all."

"It could have been," she said, following him to the door.

He put on his raincoat. "Did you really marry him?"

"Not yet. But I suppose I will. Now that I can support his bookie."

He pressed her shoulder. "Good luck. You might have been making it up as you went along but I think you've got that break coming anyway."

In front of the building, his watch said 9:45. He walked over to Fifth Avenue to get a cab but the first half dozen to skim by were loaded because of the wet streets. He finally got one going the wrong way and climbed in. He told the cabbie, "The Waldorf and don't spare the overdrive if you want to save a beautiful friendship."

"Okay, buddy," the driver said, "but we gotta go two blocks before we can turn right."

"I want everything nice and legal," McGann said. It was 9:54.

They crossed Madison as the light turned red and swung south in Park. At the hotel, they whined around the mid-street island and slid to the door. The meter said fifty-five cents and McGann gave him a dollar. It was 9:58.

"Nice saving," McGann said.

"She must be a beautiful friend," the driver said. "I had one like that myself onct."

"To each his own," McGann said, and went in, taking the steps up to the lobby two at a time. He called Chary's room on a house phone and she answered almost immediately. He said, "I suppose I'm way too early."

"You just got under the wire and you know it," she said. "I'll be right down."

McGann strolled over toward the Lexington Avenue elevators. There was a wall mirror there and he paused to adjust Tompkins' tie but one look in the glass drove all minor matters from his mind. Flaming across his shirt collar where the face of Irma Nelson had nestled was a bright pink smear.

He was scrabbling frantically for a handkerchief when Chary Jones spoke behind him. "And they say women are vain."

"They got me," McGann groaned and turned around.

20
ON THE TOWN

Slowly, the smile faded from her lips. "What's that on your collar?" she said. "As if I didn't know."

"Collar?" McGann said. "What collar?" He touched it and tried to look down. "Must be blood. I've had an eventful evening."

"Obviously. For heaven's sake, don't rub it." She led him to one side and took out a compact, powdering the mark. "One thing I draw the line at is going out with a man whose collar doesn't match my lipstick."

"I can explain everything."

"You don't have to."

"But I want to. Irma Nelson collapsed on my manly bosom and I gave her what comfort I could. It was the decent thing to do."

"Of course," she said. She took his arm and they started down the long steps to Lexington Avenue. "We're very Joe College tonight. Where's your hat?"

"Hat?"

"Yes, hat."

"I left it on Kathleen Rogers' radiator."

She stopped with one foot poised. "You left it on whose what?"

"The radiator. Kathleen Rogers'. To dry. It was wet."

"This is wonderful," she said. "I feel flattered to think my number finally came up. Who punched you in the eye?"

"That," McGann said, "is a badge of purest courage. Received in deadly combat. From Hooker Hunyak."

"You're sure it wasn't Gypsy Rose Lee when she caught you hiding in her dressing room?"

"Word of honor. Anything else, Mr. District Attorney?"

"Only that you're wearing a lovely tie. Unusual figure, too. I gave Ronnie one just like it."

McGann assayed a light laugh. "To tell the truth, I borrowed it. Thought it went well with the eye."

"My God," Chary said. "On top of everything else, he's a ghoul." She faced him on the sidewalk. "It's too late to back out now. Let's start with El Morocco but please don't try to take any pandas away from anybody there."

They had three drinks and two dances at El Morocco and went on to the Stork where they had two drinks and three dances. In the Versailles, Chary finally smiled. McGann had two drinks and she had her fortune told. At Leon & Eddie's, McGann had three drinks and Chary ordered scrambled eggs.

"Don't you think you'd better eat?" she asked.

"Eat?" McGann said. "Solids?" He looked pained. "You mean I should ruin a million-dollar edge with two million dollars worth of food?"

"I thought it might be a good idea."

He leaned forward. "Hunger stalks the land. One third of the nation is ill-fed and yet—and yet—you would have me snatch the scrambled eggs from the very lips of the deserving." For emphasis he struck the table sharply with a swizzle-stick, which promptly broke. "Never let it be said that a McGann violated foodless Monday. Difficult as it—"

"It's Tuesday now," Chary said. "It's a quarter after Tuesday." She signaled the waiter. "Better make that two orders of scrambled eggs."

"I knew it was a mistake to give them the vote," McGann told the waiter.

"Yes, sir."

"Next thing you know they'll want to throw away their veils."

"I'm afraid so, sir."

He addressed the waiter's disappearing back. "They'll be painting their faces and sitting in saloons. The barber shops will be invaded. Man's last—"

"Let's dance," Chary said.

"Can I lead?" McGann asked humbly.

It was over the coffee that she said, "Look who's coming in."

He turned and peered through the low-hanging smoke, past the bar to the door. A pallid dome moved at the side of a fragile blonde as Attorney Amos Holton gallantly handed Gladys Mars to a table.

"Hey, hey," McGann said. "That's getting to be a big production number."

"Won't he be angry to find you here? I mean aren't you supposed to be out following people and things like that?"

"I'm working every minute." He caught her look and added quickly, "Thinking."

"Excuse me," she said and rose, and he stood up, too. He watched the annoyed set of her back as she disappeared toward the powder room. When he went over to Holton's table, the two looked up with well-concealed pleasure.

"Hello, there," McGann said genially. "Small Fifty-Second Street."

"How'ja do," Gladys Mars said.

"Ah, McGann," Holton said, without rising. His face was expressionless. "I don't wish to discuss business here but I'd like to see you in the morning. I have been in touch this evening with Inspector O'Callahan and he expects shortly to clear up this entire unfortunate affair."

"Marvelous," McGann said. "Mrs. O'Callahan is bound to be pleased. Meanwhile, though, there's one thing I'd like to have."

"What's that?"

"The record Mr. Tompkins made of his will. I'd like to hear it again without so many people around."

A cloud passed over Holton's face. "I wish you had spoken earlier," he said. "Mr. Farwell asked for it to add to his collection of unique recordings. It has no legal status, you know— that's all taken care of in the written will—so I let him have it."

McGann glanced toward the powder room, then back to the table. "I'll borrow it from Frazier," he said. "Did he pick it up in person?"

"Pearson said he'd drop it off." Briefly, the lawyer explained that the former butler had been in his office discussing final details of his legacy when Farwell's telephone request had come through. "He knew Mr. Farwell, of course, and seemed anxious to do the favor."

Chary was threading her way back to the table. "Thanks," McGann said. "I'll check it."

They reached the table together and she let him push in her chair without smiling. McGann beckoned the waiter over and said, "The national debt, please." He asked her. "Like to see a disc jockey going into the stretch?"

She had seemed suddenly tired but now her interest quickened. "Frazier? Are we going to see him? Why?"

"I want to borrow something from him—that will record, to be exact." He looked at his watch. "He should be weighing-in now. The studio's just over around Eighth Avenue."

"Don't I know," she said. "There's a chair dedicated to me in the waiting room."

"That's right, you did brighten the air waves a few times, didn't you?" He gave the waiter a bill. "Hope this doesn't put you in too high a bracket."

"Thanks," the waiter said. "I'll risk it."

Midtown was still in its stride, crowds coming and going before the neon-lighted bistros. They streamed across the corners against the lights while the taxi inched its way through. Snatches of off-key song and brittle laughter floated through the cab window and when they stopped for the light at Seventh Avenue three sailors thrust grinning faces against the glass to peer at Chary.

"Hiya, beautiful!" they shouted happily.

"Stand by to repel a boarding party," McGann said. "All hands to stations on the double."

The taxi started again and the sailors gave it a farewell pounding on the back. "A broadside," he said, "right in the taillight but I think we made it."

"They're sweet," Chary said.

The doorman at the radio studio knew her and said, "Sure" when they asked to go up. They walked along quiet corridors, entered a large room filled with folding chairs. Music was coming from a loudspeaker and through a glass partition at the end of the room they could see Frazier Farwell. An engineer wearing headphones was at the mixing controls.

Farwell was sideways to them. He had his jacket off and his collar was open. He turned away, not seeing them, and hunching up to the microphone as they came forward. His voice sounded over the speaker in the room as it was being broadcast.

"Here we are back in our 'Can You Imagine' ballroom," he told his unseen listeners, dropping in the inevitable chuckle. "There's a big crowd as usual this morning and I'm going to ask this girl and her escort to step up to the mike and tell us what in the world they see in each other."

He slid into the act with professional ease—first as the girl, giggling self-consciously. "Really, Mr. Farwell, I don't see too well. We were afraid once it was that eye trouble—gloccamorra.

Oh, you mean why do I like Ellsworth, here? Well, he's so strong and so silent . . ."

"Is that true, Ellsworth?" Farwell said in his natural voice and switched instantly to the fictitious "escort," who said, "Duh?" "Thank you very much, Ellsworth," Farwell said. "You can go back in your barrel now while we hear the Columbia record Abe Lyman made of 'You're The Cream In My Coffee' way back when people could afford it." His index finger made a short arc in the direction of the engineer and immediately the jumpy rhythm beat out into the room.

"He's even worse than I thought he was," McGann said.

"I think Frazier's very talented," Chary said. She waved a gloved hand as Farwell turned and the disc jockey's face lit up with pleasure. He made a signal to the engineer and came over and opened the door of the glass cubicle.

"Hiya, folks," he said. "This is an unexpected. Care to say a few words which will be carried into every hamburger joint east of the Pecos?"

"Not me," McGann said. "I'm holding out for a guest shot with Phil Spitalny. Maybe Chary would."

She was smiling at Farwell with unusual warmth and Mc-Gann decided that she was still mad at him. He knew it when she put her hand on Frazier's arm and turned the charm on high. "I'd rather just listen to the master," she said. "Do that takeoff on Arthur Godfrey doing a takeoff on Galen Drake."

"Oh, that," Farwell said modestly.

"No, do it. You're wonderful on that."

McGann leaned against the wall and decided that nothing short of an attack of acute appendicitis would enable him to get back into the conversation. The music suddenly ended and Farwell slipped back to the microphone, picking up the tale of his mythical ballroom with practiced nonchalance. He did the takeoff on the takeoff while Chary registered delight at him through the glass. Then he announced a medley of three numbers, which McGann knew would give them a chance to talk. Farwell came out again and turned down the speaker.

"That was simply terrific," Chary gushed, while Farwell looked pleased.

Oh, no, you don't, McGann thought, and jumped in with both feet. "I want to borrow that will record Tompkins made," he said. "Holton told me he let you have it for your collection."

Farwell looked bewildered. "But I didn't get it."

"He sent it to you this afternoon."

Farwell shook his head and ran thin fingers nervously through his yellow hair. "Holton promised I could have it but it didn't arrive. I figured I'd have to pick it up."

"Pearson was supposed to bring it to you."

A light dawned in Farwell's eyes. "That ozonated Jeeves," he said. "That bird-baiting butler. He'd steal a worm from the first robin."

"He never delivered the record, then?"

"If he's gone south with that item," Farwell said, "I'll run him to Patagonia. Why do you realize—"

"You won't have to chase him that far," McGann said. "He's stopping in Jamaica to refuel. I'll take the short cut and head him off at the pass."

The engineer was waving frantically to Farwell. "Gotta get back to the mine," he said. "Can you stick around?" He ducked in before they could answer and was hardly back at the microphone when a young messenger came through the room. The messenger had a length of yellow teletype paper in his hand. He glanced at McGann and then slowed up, giving Chary both barrels. When he finally went inside he thrust the teletype before Farwell and continued to stare back at her. McGann turned the speaker up again.

". . . the boys and girls in the ballroom," Farwell was saying, and stopped, scanning the message. "We interrupt this broadcast," he said, "to bring you a special bulletin from our news room." There was a curious timbre in his voice and he looked out at them with a drawn face.

"Police tonight sounded an eight-state alarm for the apprehension of Dinkman 'Dink' Wexton, a New York newspaperman, in connection with the recent murder of Ronald Tompkins. Wexton, an intimate of the slain copper-heir, is wanted for questioning in several newly-uncovered phases of the investigation, according to Deputy Inspector Cornelius O'Callahan."

"Dink!" Chary gasped.

"They're crazy," McGann said. He took Chary's arm and signaled that they were going. Farwell had started his sacred commercial and spread his hands helplessly. "That's why I'm going to ask you right now to send in your check to the Book-of-the-Hour Club," he intoned. "You will receive by return mail—and in a plain wrapper—that passionate, pulsating novel of a Yankee heart aflame on foreign shores—'The Sultan From Salem'!"

"Go-ing," McGann mouthed, pointing to the outer door.

Farwell grimaced and held up a fistful of typewritten pages. "When a man from Mass meets a maid whose only code is Love," he said desperately, "no harem can hold her. And don't let anybody hold you from sitting down right now and writing out that check. I repeat—"

"Let's go," McGann said. "Some of these commercials are longer than the books."

"All right," Chary said. The false gaiety had fled. Her eyes were inexpressibly weary. "What do you suppose they'll do to Dink?"

"They've got to find him first."

"What are you going to do now?"

"I've got to figure a few angles," McGann said evasively. "Will you do something for me?"

"What?"

"Go back to the hotel. Stay there like you did before and get some rest. I'll call you."

He signaled a cab and it swerved over and he put her in. "The Waldorf," he said, thrusting a bill at the driver. He smiled at her through the window but her face was set. The cab pulled away and in a minute he got another one. He gave the driver the address of his East 47th Street garage and bounced back against the leather as it leaped forward.

The attendant brought the convertible out. "Anybody been looking for me tonight?" McGann asked. "Especially a little guy in an accordion-pleated hat?"

"Not a soul, Mr. McGann."

McGann slid behind the wheel. "I'm not sure he has one," he said. "I'll settle for the mortal husk." He swung over toward Third and headed for his office.

21
BLOCK THAT BUTLER!

McGann pushed a dashboard button and the convertible top slid soundlessly up and into place. He turned south under the steel network of the Third Avenue elevated, and switched on the radio. In a moment, Frazier Farwell was saying urgently, ". . . now. Tomorrow may be too late to take advantage of this wonderful offer." He paused, and when he resumed McGann could detect the relief in his voice. "Here's a version of Canadian Capers that Ted Weems did back in 1934 . . ."

He turned the music down low, the thin whistling of Elmo Tanner barely sounding above the drumming of the tires on the rough paving blocks. There were few people about in this neighborhood and the only lights besides the street lamps were from the taverns. McGann turned into 42nd Street, past the skyscraper housing his office, driving slowly to spot the passersby.

Several taxis jockeyed toward the light and DPW men in gray uniforms were feeding ashcans into their huge gray truck banging them back onto the sidewalk—but there was no sign of Wexton.

McGann drove on to his apartment, peering into the foyer, and then circling the block with no better luck. What his unofficial assistant had been up to to draw an eight-state alarm, he could not imagine. But he was reasonably certain that Wexton would be trying to find him.

He cruised back to 42nd Street and was going on to telephone *The Blade* city desk from a tavern when he saw a thin figure in a topcoat and battered hat emerge from Grand Central Station. Wexton glanced back over his shoulder and started hurriedly across the street half a block beyond McGann.

In a moment a heavyset figure flung out of the station, paused for a quick look around and started after the reporter. Wexton broke into a run. McGann switched off his lights and stamped on the accelerator. The convertible leaped forward and at the same moment McGann leaned on the horn.

The detective pursuing Wexton halted abruptly in the middle of the street, then leaped back as the blaring, sightless car bore down. Up ahead, the reporter was setting a new track record to Lexington Avenue. McGann swerved toward the curb, threw open the door and yelled, "Dink!"

He had picked up to fifty again before the reporter had the door closed. They heard the shrill blast of a police whistle, followed instantly by a shot. McGann tore through Lexington and Third Avenues against the lights, whining north in Second.

"He's caught a cab," Wexton said, looking back as they turned. "Bet the big slob never pays for it."

McGann let the car out until it seemed to be traveling approximately six inches above the pavement. The lights of the following cab danced in his mirror now, two tiny bulbs down the black canyon.

"Railroad cop?" he asked.

"Naw, East Fifty-First," Wexton said.

The convertible shrieked as McGann braked and lurched east again. "Can't keep this up long," McGann said. "We'll pick up a radio car sure as hell."

There was a chance that the pursuers had not seen where the darkened car turned off. McGann made the short run to Roosevelt Drive and doubled back. It was wide and smooth and they spun over it silently. "I'll always love Franklin for this roadbed," Wexton said. "Plus the fact that he got reporters' police cards out of their shoes and back in their hats."

Two cars were speeding south in the next lane and just ahead of them. There was about sixty feet between them. McGann switched his lights on again and shot into the hole. The three sped along like innocent triplets. McGann turned the radio up in time to hear Farwell sign off and then he switched it to police short wave.

". . . Lookout for a black limousine believed to contain four men armed with machine guns," the police announcer said. "No license number. These men are helping the escape of Dinkman 'Dirk' Wexton, wanted in connection . . ."

"Get WQXR," Wexton said. "Music to lam by. It's so restful."

McGann clicked it off. There was no further sight of the taxicab and they continued south between their protective escorts. Once a radio car with its white-painted hood passed them going in the opposite direction and Wexton slid down in the seat but it made no move to follow.

Off to their left the East River glittered darkly with lights from the Queens side and then they were passing the sprawling buildings of Stuyvesant Town. "Get down to South Street," Wexton advised. "I know a place where we can reconnoiter."

McGann said, "Do they have a house rule against strangling nitwits?"

"All I can say is that going through O'Callahan's desk seemed like a good idea at the time. How'd I know the cleaning woman was a stool pigeon?"

They parked the car half a block away on South Street and went into a little bar near the Seaman's Institute. A couple of men in short jackets looked them over curiously and turned back to their drinks. There were half a dozen tables in the rear and at one a thin, lantern-jawed man had fallen asleep. His seaman's cap had slipped from his sandy hair.

They picked a table as far away from him as possible and after a while the bartender walked over. "What'll it be?"

"Singapore sling," Wexton said moodily. "I might as well start getting used to the place."

"Two beers," McGann corrected. When they were brought he eyed Wexton sternly. "I hope you were worth rescuing."

"Smartest investment you ever made," the reporter said. He pulled a soiled envelope from his pocket and began studying the chicken tracks scrawled across it.

"Six months ago," he translated, "the Stanton dame passed out in a West Side fleabag. Tompkins' name and number were in her purse. The manager smelled dough and called Ronnie without notifying anybody else. Tompkins hushed it up and had her straightened out at an upstate sanitarium."

"Her first trouble with drugs?"

"Yes. When the stuff about her murder came out in the papers the manager told the beat cop on a promise that there wouldn't be any trouble. He was allowed to make an unofficial statement."

"He would have been a sad sack if she had died then," McGann said. "The narcotics boys like a chance to question them on their source of supply."

"Bet that gets them a lot."

"It doesn't work very often," McGann admitted. "In the back of addicts' minds is always the thought that they might want to start up again and they don't want to cut themselves off for good. They usually say they meet a guy named Joe on a corner somewhere."

"Stanton was never even questioned."

"And of course she wasn't cured, either. Probably walked out as soon as she felt better."

"I don't know," Wexton said. "That was the best thing I found in O'Callahan's desk, next to a picture of a babe in a bathing suit and a ticket to the Irish sweepstakes. It was signed 'Manhattan Mabel'."

"The sweepstakes ticket?"

"No, the picture."

"My God," McGann said. "No wonder he sent out an alarm for you." He was really startled. "You're hotter than a two-bit meerschaum. I hope you didn't take them."

The reporter grinned crookedly. "I wouldn't do a thing like that. I just fixed Mabel up with a goatee. It gave her a lot more character."

McGann looked apprehensively toward the door. "Then he hides in the information booth at Grand Central," he said. "Why didn't you try climbing a lamppost in Times Square?"

"If you'd stay in your office and work once in a while I'd have been all right," Wexton said. "I had to see a man about a caboose. So who's on the track right next to me but the law." He chuckled evilly in recollection. "I got out of there so fast I think I melted my zipper."

McGann shook his head and hauled out the notebook, flipping through it to the middle. "If they catch you we'll plead that it's a case of where the mind leaves the body." He turned back a page. "I want to find Ambrose Pearson."

"He's in Jamaica. What do you want him for?"

McGann explained about the record, with which the butler apparently had disappeared. "He was in town late yesterday so maybe he didn't go back. I'd hate to drive all the way out there unless I had to."

Wexton suggested a telephone check and offered the information that Pearson had a brother named Otto in Jamaica. "He used to bend my ear about what a no-good Otto was but he probably moved in with him when they had to leave Ronnie's."

McGann took the empty glasses to the bar and ordered two more beers. He asked for a Queens telephone book and the bartender dug a dog-eared copy out of a cabinet. They found O. A. Pearson, Oscar Pearson and Otto Pearson. McGann copied the number and called it from the booth in the rear.

A man answered in a voice which indicated what he thought of being awakened at a quarter to three. "Ambrose ain't here," he growled, "and it's a hell of a time to be calling up."

McGann spoke rapidly to forestall a banging receiver. "I'm calling for Attorney Holton," he said. "I know it's late but we just found out that Mr. Tompkins wanted to leave some money to Ambrose's relatives, too. I have to reach him to get all their names."

When the man at the other end had had time to recover, he sounded considerably mollified. "Well, you can start with Otto, his brother," he said. "That's me."

"Really? Congratulations!"

"How much is it?"

"How much? Why, we're not sure just yet. Where did you say Ambrose is?"

Otto gave an address on Perry Street in Greenwich Village. "It's my sister's," he said. "Louella. Put her down, too." He paused. "If you want me to, I can come in right now."

"That won't be necessary," McGann said. "We'll send out an armored truck at dawn."

He hung up and went back to the table. "Ambrose stayed over," he said, and explained what he had learned. "We'd better get over there. I'm just hoping that record's still in one piece."

Wexton was wide-eyed. "You mean Pearson might smash it? What's so important about it?"

McGann pushed back his chair. "It'll be more helpful than vital," he said. "I just expect it to corroborate something I've got in mind."

"You're so clear," Wexton complained. "I suppose this stuff I found out doesn't matter again. It's only my neck."

"No, it fits in very nicely. Very nicely. It probably will win you your Junior G-Man badge."

"That's more like it. If you'd pulled that 'never thought much of it anyway' gag I'd have slugged you."

"You might as well," McGann said, thinking of Hunyak, "everybody else has."

McGann paid for the beers, and they stood just inside the door for a minute, casing the street. The bartender walked over and kicked the chair of the sleeping seaman. "C'mon, George," he ordered. "You're due on board."

"That guy sailed before his ship," Wexton observed. "I want him on the bridge of my yacht next time I go around the Horn."

McGann seemed satisfied about the situation in the street. "Let's go." They stepped out into the darkness of South Street, across from the shadowy hulks of freighters. They approached the car warily, even walking past it once to make sure that it wasn't being watched. Satisfied, they retraced their steps swiftly and slid in.

McGann wheeled up Greenwich Avenue. There was still plenty of life in the Village. Couples stood in front of nightclubs and the white front coffee pots were filled. They found the address on Perry Street and again parked the car a short distance from the building which they were entering.

A dim bulb burned in the tiny foyer but they were able to find "L. Pearson" on the broken mailboxes. McGann pressed the button, hearing a faint ring above, and they went up when they found that the door latch was not working. A woman whose gray hair was caught up in paper curlers stuck her head from a second-floor door. She looked like a decorated turtle ready to snap its head back in at the first alarm. "What do you want?" she demanded suspiciously.

"Otto told us that we'd find Ambrose here," McGann said. To allay her fears, he had stopped several steps from the door. "It's important. About Mr. Tompkins."

The lineup of names seemed to calm and impress her. "Just a minute." She closed the door and they heard the lock catch.

"Maybe I ought to cover the outside," Wexton whispered.

McGann shook his head. He said, "She asked for a minute and that's what we'll give them. Then we'll wake up the building."

But no more than thirty seconds had ticked by when they heard the shuffle of approaching footsteps and the door again opened. Pearson looked at them with eyes full of fear. "The detective," he said. "And Mr. Wexton. But what is it?"

"We want to talk to you, Pearson," McGann said shortly. "We'll come in."

They pushed past the butler, who had pulled a short blue robe over a nightshirt which flapped about his bare shanks. There was a light on in the small living room filled with heavy, old furniture. They faced him there. "I want that record," McGann said.

Pearson tugged at the robe cord with shaking hands. "I knew I shouldn't have done it," he whimpered. "I knew it. But I just couldn't resist it." He gazed at them imploringly. "Believe me, gentlemen, it was my first crime. On my word—"

Wexton had his neck out like one of the butler's feathered friends spotting a grub. "Holy smokes!" he said. He stared at McGann. "A confession. He done it!"

Even McGann was looking queerly at the butler. He said sharply, "What crime?"

Pearson seemed ready to collapse. "Thievery," he moaned. "I admit it. I was going to keep it. In fifteen years with Mr. Tompkins, gentlemen, it is the only thing outside of an occasional bottle of spirits which the master never missed. On my oath—"

"Get it," McGann said.

Pearson tottered to the hall closet and dragged a worn briefcase from the shelf. For a moment he fumbled with the catches, then suddenly he pulled the record out with quivering fingers. It gleamed warmly in the lamplight as he thrust it at them. "Take it," he quavered. "Take it. I never meant—"

Four things happened almost simultaneously in the next split-second: Pearson's unsure foot caught on the rug, the record sailed through the air like a black discus, McGann yelled, "Heads up!" and the leading edge clipped Wexton across the Adam's Apple. The record dropped unharmed into his outstretched hands.

McGann grabbed it. "Good boy!" he said. "Help Mr. Pearson up."

Wexton made strangling noises. His fists were clenched. "It's got to stop," he said. "This is positively the last time."

McGann was inspecting the disc. It was cut on only one side and bore no identification label in the center. Pearson had gained his feet amid profuse apologies. McGann cut him off. "Is there a record player here?"

"Oh, no, sir. I'd ordered one for home."

"Never mind," McGann said. "We'll take it along. Come on, Dink." He paused to pick up the briefcase and glance through it, then eyed the ex-butler. "You're sure this is the right one? You wouldn't slip me a ringer?"

"That's the one Mr. Holton gave me to deliver," Pearson said fervently. He hopped sideways to the door as they went out. "It was just that it was the master's own voice, sir. I was fascinated when I learned it existed." He was almost weeping. "Mr. Tompkins was always kind to me. There won't be any more trouble, will there, sir? I give you my sacred—"

McGann stopped at the door. "Go back to bed, Mr. Pearson, and don't say anything about this to anyone." He smiled. "You're as safe as a swallow in a barn." He tapped the record. "I may even be able to get you a copy."

Murmurs of "Thank you, sir" followed them down the stairs. Wexton said, "You want me to hold that while you see if the coast is clear?"

"I'll see if the coast is clear and I'll hold onto this, too," Mc-Gann said. "I hope I never have to live through another minute like that with you and Buttles batting this thing back and forth. You'd think it was the check."

"Di Maggio never made a better catch," Wexton boasted.

McGann stepped out and immediately stepped back in. "Radio car," he said. They flattened against the wall on either side of the door and in a moment the police car drove leisurely past. McGann counted ten and they slipped out, walking with purpose but unhurriedly to the convertible.

As they turned north, Wexton suggested, "There's an all-night music store on Broadway where you can run it off."

"I've got a little player at home," McGann said. "One tube and six needles. We'll hear it there if O'Callahan doesn't jump out when we lift the lid."

They circled the apartment building twice, left the car down the block and went in. McGann pulled the shades before turning on the lights. He got out the record player and blew dust from the top. Wexton said, "That looks like a model Edison abandoned."

"Old Faithful," McGann said. "I used to play soft numbers on this and lovely young things leaned on me like hollyhocks in a high wind."

He plugged it in and in a moment a faint hum came on. Swiftly, he slipped the record to the turntable, clicked it on and lowered the needle. He said, "Take it away, Ronnie."

22
"GOODBYE AGAIN"

"Good evening," Ronnie Tompkins said, exactly as he had before. He chuckled. *"You weren't expecting me tonight, were you? But you know I'd rather die than miss a party."*

Wexton started to say something but McGann waved him to silence. He sat on a chair hunched up close to the speaker and now he rested his chin on his hand and closed his eyes in concentration.

"At one time or another, all of you meant something rather special to me. You were grifters mostly, playing 'Good Time Ronnie' for what was in it. But don't look like that. I wasn't fooled and I loved you for what you were."

The smooth voice flowed into the room, filling it with gentle sarcasm, changing abruptly to bitter recriminations and back to unctuous patronage. McGann sat motionless, following the macabre monologue.

"Go on, now, with your party, my friends and my loves."

Once more the low, self-satisfied laugh. *"I'm with you, you know. I'm here."*

McGann leaned over and shut it off, sitting for a moment with his hand on the control. When he looked at Wexton the reporter seemed to have grown a shade paler. "You talked with

189

Tompkins a hundred times," McGann said. "How'd he sound to you there?"

"His pixiest," Wexton said. "Having fun, and he didn't really have fun very often. But it would take a gag like that to tickle him."

McGann rose. "That does it then," he said. He went over and got his cigarettes from his raincoat pocket and flicked the match to a tray. He added thoughtfully, "It'll be a damned hard thing to prove."

"Either quit talking in riddles or give me the combination to the icebox," Wexton said. "Better still, do both."

"One turn to the right," McGann said. "Don't touch anything that's moving."

The hour before dawn was deathly quiet. A palpable stillness hung over the city, the building, made itself felt in the room. McGann smoked and paced restlessly, lost in thought. Wexton munched a sandwich and drank beer from a bottle. They both jumped when the telephone rang.

"Probably Otto," Wexton said, "trying to get even."

McGann reached the instrument in three strides. "Hello." There was a muted buzzing. "Hello," he said again and this time Chary spoke. Her voice sounded faint and far away, and there was a sob in it.

"I'm sorry," she said. "You won't see me again." There was a pause and the tears broke through. "It will be better this way. I don't know what happened to me . . . really I don't . . ."

"Listen, Chary," McGann said. "Listen to me. Are you at the hotel now? I'll—"

"Just far away," she said. "Don't ask me where. Far enough that no one will ever find me . . . ever . . ."

McGann swung on Wexton. "There's a pay phone in the lobby. Get down there and trace this call. I'll hold the line open as long as I can."

The door slammed behind the reporter and McGann flinched. If there was one time he didn't want neighbors pounding on the wall this was it. Chary's voice still came over the line. She was weeping openly now. "Sometimes things happen . . . and people do things they never dreamed they would . . . or could . . ."

"Listen to me," McGann said once more and then he gave up trying to break in, listening instead to the tragic singsong that droned on almost as if she were explaining something to herself.

"Being sorry doesn't do any good, does it? It sounds so useless . . . and yet that's all there is to say . . . except goodbye." The receiver clicked down.

"Hello!" McGann flashed rapidly. "Hello!" The operator came on. "What number are you calling, please?"

"I'm not calling any number; somebody was calling me."

"I'm sorry," the operator said, "your party has hung up."

"Can you get them back?"

"No, sir."

"Never mind." McGann held down the cradle cutoff for a moment, got the dial tone. The wheel whirled as he dialed ELdorado 5-3000. On the second ring the girl came on, "Waldorf-Astoria." McGann gave Chary's room number. "One moment, please." She closed the key and McGann waited impatiently, the phone growing moist in his hand.

She came back, "Are you calling Mary Jones?"

"Yes, it's an emer—" She was gone again. McGann swore under his breath. The key flicked open. "I will give you the room clerk, sir."

"I don't want—"

"Room Clerk speaking."

McGann got hold of himself with an effort. "This is very important. I'm trying to reach Miss Mary Jones." He repeated the room number.

"Miss Jones has checked out."

"Checked out? When?"

A pause. "About an hour ago."

"Was she with anybody?"

"I beg pardon?"

"Did anybody come to the hotel for her? Did she leave with anyone, or did she go out alone?"

The room clerk apparently was trying to think back. "I'm quite certain she was alone when she left the lobby, sir."

Wexton flung back into the room. He was panting. "No good." McGann told the room clerk, "Just a minute," and turned to the reporter. "They said the connection was broken too soon," Wexton explained.

McGann nodded, returned to the phone. "This may be a matter of life or death. Did Miss Jones give any hint to where she was going?"

"Not to us, sir."

McGann's voice was steady. "Listen carefully," he said. "Talk to the doorman. Find out if he overheard her instructions to a cab driver. Or see if he remembers what cab she took so it can be traced. If I can't locate her another way I'll call you back. Will you do that?"

The clerk sounded dubious. "This is all very irregular, you know. Just who is this calling?"

Patiently, McGann explained about Chary's connection with the slain Ronnie Tompkins. "I had her stay there as a safety measure. You see what this means?"

"I'll do what I can, sir," the clerk said briskly. "I'll get the house officer on it right away."

"Thanks." He dropped the receiver, started for the door. "Come on," he told Wexton, "I think I know where that call came from."

"Where in hell is she?"

They clattered down the stairs, gained the street. "It's a chance but a good one," McGann said. "Tompkins' place." They reached the car on a dead run, jumped in. "What would she be doing there?" Wexton asked. "Returning to the scene of the—" He choked off, surprise at his own thought in his face as the car lunged forward.

McGann didn't answer the last question. Instead, he said, "Now that we'll want a radio car, I'll bet we don't raise one."

They spun north in Lexington, jockeyed over to Madison, whining through the city locked at last in that quiet moment between the final revelry and the first milkman. The slick streets unwound rapidly in the headlights, and twice McGann wrenched the car around other machines poking out into the thoroughfare.

They flashed into the Sixties and he slowed up to shriek protestingly into Tompkins' block. The car skidded, lurching into the curb as they pulled up. Above them the house loomed gloomy and forbidding.

"Dark as a mole's rumpus room," Wexton said. "You guessed wrong."

"Around the back," McGann said, "and quiet."

They ducked into the adjoining service entrance, coming out in the rear courtyard. A glance showed a faint, flickering light behind the drawn shades of the study. Wexton said, "I'll be a son-of-a—" when a hard hand clapped over his mouth and McGann pulled him close to the building.

McGann put his mouth close to the reporter's ear. "I'll boost you up so you can pull down the fire-escape extension. Easy does it. Once you're up there, watch and wait. I'll go around the front. Got it?"

Wexton reached up and pulled the hand away, then nodded wordlessly. McGann leading, they edged silently along the building Once McGann leaned out to look up. The dancing light was still there but he could see nothing else. Across the way the windows of Kathleen Rogers' apartment were black.

An upper wind had cleared the sky, driving the last wisps from the stars, and McGann could see the end of the counterbalanced extension. He drew Wexton forward and hooked his hands together in front. "Put one hand against the building," he whispered, "then step up on my shoulders. When you get hold of it, bring it down slow."

The reporter's left shoe pressed down on his hooked hands. McGann straightened his knees. Wexton got hold of the back of his head and McGann lifted and he was up. He teetered there uncertainly until McGann got a grip just above his ankles. When Wexton was steady, he eased out from the wall toward the iron tracery.

McGann could tell from Wexton's movements when the reporter had gotten hold. He hoped the extension was still as muffled as the other time he had used it. A careful glance upward showed that it was coming down under Wexton's pressure. McGann reached up with one hand and held it head high while Wexton slid softly forward.

He tapped Wexton's ankle and motioned him ahead and now he held it up with both hands while the reporter crept along. It was not until the reporter was almost at the runway leading to the study windows that he released the extension and let it rise slowly into place again.

McGann moved quickly along the building and through to the front. He experienced the weird feeling that once before he had done exactly this same thing. Only now he had two keys to the house of marriage and mystery.

There was not a person in sight as he slipped up the stairs. This time he was able to forestall the clicking lock and reach the pitch dark hall. He took a slow breath, held it. Looking down its length he could see no light now in the study. The door was closed. He had left it open.

His feet made no sound on the thick rug, his outstretched fingers trailed along the wall, touched the door to the art gallery. It had been locked. Eyes straining, one hand ahead and the other on the wall, he moved ahead.

Now he could hear the crackle of the fire in the study. The temporary door, he remembered, had not been as sturdy as the original. As his fingers touched the knob, there came to him the hint of a sweet and cloying odor.

The scent drove thoughts of caution from his mind. He called, "Chary!" once, the sound echoing eerily in the corridor and up the staircase, and tried to turn the knob. It held. He lunged heavily and the flimsy partition gave way.

She lay stretched on the spot where Ronnie Tompkins' blood had drained. The firelight was mirrored in her outflung hair and her eyes were closed. Across her mouth and nostrils lay a thick white cloth and the odor of chloroform lay heavy in the room.

McGann took a step forward and paused. On the table next to the chair where he had sat for that first interview stood another glass. A fresh cigarette had been crushed out in the tray.

From the tray in the middle of Tompkins' desk, smoke still rose.

A movement in the far corner swung his gaze slowly in that direction. The door to the servants' stairway stood ajar, a black slit, and as he watched it, it widened gradually.

Frazier Farwell glided into the room. He held a black automatic close in front of him, the bore on a level with McGann's stomach, and an evil smile lay on his lips. McGann met the eyes that drilled into his with full knowledge. Farwell's pupils had shrunk to pinpoints. The calm of powerful drugs showed in the unwavering muzzle of the gun.

"You couldn't just let it go, could you?" Farwell said. His tone was on a single key, the voice thick. "They would have said she killed herself because she was sorry for what she had done. Everything would have been forgotten then. Everyone would have been happy. But you couldn't just let it go. Oh, no. Not you."

McGann looked into the tiny eyes, not moving. He said quietly, "More killing won't get you out of this. You're a dead man. Let the girl go."

The muzzle came up a fraction of an inch. "We're all dead now," Farwell said. He chuckled, changing his voice and McGann felt a cold chill as Ronnie Tompkins seemed to speak. "I want you to prevent my murder, Mr. McGann," he said mockingly. "But, of course, I asked you to do that once before and you failed. Now you can't even prevent your own!"

The glass of the study window shattered as Wexton came through with the flying splinters. Farwell whirled and the crash of the gun blotted out the shivery tinkle. McGann's left hand closed on the hot barrel, wrenching it free with a single twist. The pinpoint pupils shot one fearful look into his and then McGann felt his right fist lashing out and the crunch of jawbone against knuckles.

Farwell bounced off the wall and crumpled crazily McGann gave him a single glance, stepped over Wexton, who still lay where he had fallen, and knelt beside Chary. A movement flung aside the deadly cloth and then he had her in his arms at the open window where the fresh breeze tore the fumes from their faces and the stars dimmed in the first streaks of light.

23
FULLER EXPLANATION DEPARTMENT

Dink Wexton finished talking to rewrite and put the phone back on Tompkins' desk. He fixed McGann with a stern eye. "Twenty minutes," he said. "That's all I ask. Then you can call anybody you want."

McGann grinned. "Fair enough—if Chary feels all right."

"I'm fine now," she said.

He was holding the automatic down at his side, and he walked over and kicked one of the logs in the fireplace so that it blazed up brightly. Frazier Farwell slumped in the chair in the corner. His shirt collar was open and his hands were bound behind him with his necktie. He didn't look up.

The windows brightened with arriving day. The first takes of Wexton's story would be through the desk now, chattering linotypes would be working on it. *The Blade* would be standing on its head, a gaping hole waiting for the replate.

Minutes ticked by. Wexton, at the desk, examined his hat and poked a pencil through the hole in the crown. He glared at the man in the corner, held it up for McGann to see. "Ruined this Stetson-type hat," he said. "With malice aforethought," he added bitterly.

Chary smiled at him gently. She was relaxed in the chair near the fire, her feet up under her, and she was still quite pale. "It'll be too small anyway, won't it? I mean saving our lives and getting the first story and all. Will they give you an Oscar?"

"Two of 'em." Wexton pushed the hat to the back of his head. "Siamese Oscars. Joined together by a belt in the back." The stereotypers could even have it now, and the pressmen standing by, ready to roll. The papers would flash out, still damp, with the banner screaming, SOLVE TOMPKINS' MURDER!

McGann had walked over to the window, looking out, with an occasional glance at the motionless figure of Farwell. He turned back to the reporter. "It's time to spoil O'Callahan's beauty sleep."

Wexton sighed. "You wouldn't consider locking this guy up in the basement and printing the confession in daily installments, would you?"

"It's a wonderful idea. But I like this part of the country." He gestured. "Do your duty."

Wexton started to dial SPring 7-3100. "It's so cozy here I hate to do this. But I guess if I don't I will never know how the hell you figured it out."

Deputy Inspector O'Callahan showed white, even teeth and pulled the chair closer to Tompkins' desk. "I hope you can prove all this," he said. "We only know for certain that Farwell shot a hole in the hat of Mr. Wexton here."

"That's a crime," McGann pointed out. "Discharging fire-arms within the city limits."

"There were extenuating circumstances." O'Callahan turned his smile on the reporter. "Wexton was in it at the time."

Dink nodded. "My friend."

McGann looked around the room. A uniformed man stood beside Farwell, whose wrists now lay handcuffed in his lap. The disc jockey gazed at them with smouldering hatred. His pupils were beginning to widen as the effect of the drug wore off. A few more hours without a dose, McGann thought, and they wouldn't be able to muffle his singing.

He said, "Stop me if I'm wrong, Frazier." He beckoned to Dink. "For the next ten minutes you're going to be Ronnie Tompkins, dead and alive. I'll play Mr. Farwell's role but I won't try the voice."

O'Callahan leaned back. "Go ahead." Chary watched quietly.

"Farwell arrived here early last Friday afternoon," McGann said. "He probably was under the influence of drugs but not so much that he didn't notice the Pearsons come out the basement door and hurry down the street. We know that they saw him.

"Ronnie Tompkins admitted Farwell to the house. I'll theorize on the next part but I feel fairly safe in it. There was a quarrel, probably over the fact that Farwell had started Shirley Stanton on the use of drugs and was using any money she could get hold of to keep them both supplied. They needed it at $3,000 an ounce in the illicit market.

"Possibly Tompkins threatened to cut them both off for good and take Shirley out of his will."

McGann stepped over to the desk and opened the upper right-hand drawer. "Tompkins' easy geniality was his own undoing. People like Farwell had unlimited opportunities to snoop around here. He knew about the gun. Half-crazy with narcotics and the fear of being cut off from an easy drug supply, he waited until Tompkins' back was turned, grabbed the gun and shot him.

"The bullet took effect in a peculiar way." McGann took Wexton by the shoulder, had him lie face down near the desk. "It killed Tompkins, all right, but it didn't penetrate his body, as the medical examiner's report showed. It was stopped by the sternum. All bleeding was internal."

O'Callahan nodded. "There was a post-mortem lividity of the left chest."

"Yes." McGann straightened. "That peculiarity of the wound became more important as other things fitted in. Anyway, Farwell undoubtedly stood here dazed for a few minutes trying to decide what to do next.

"Perhaps he expected police to come racing up when some neighbor reported the shot. If he just ran away, the Pearsons would be questioned when the body was found and reveal that Farwell was the last person known to have been with Tompkins.

"As his nerve returned, he decided that the closed windows and thick walls had deadened the shot and that it hadn't been heard. He also discovered that Tompkins had not been bleeding onto the rug. Gradually the idea formed of having the murder seem to be committed at a later time when he would have somebody with him to establish his alibi."

McGann straddled the prone reporter, slipped his hands under the arms, and pulled him toward the servants' stairway. "He put the body in here where it was closed off and exceptionally warm, being careful to keep it face down.

"Then he went about setting the stage. As an actor, with a special talent for imitating voices and mannerisms, Farwell was confident that he could fool his alibi witness into believing he was Tompkins—especially if he stayed out of the light and the witness did not know Tompkins personally."

O'Callahan's eyes were bright blue. "Why pick on you?"

"For several reasons. It was true that I headed a Federal squad that did the Tompkins' interests some good and there probably was a discussion of it at the time. Moreover, I think Tompkins was planning to call me in, maybe to watch Shirley and keep Farwell away from her. I found traces of notations on the calendar but the page itself was gone."

"I noticed that page was torn off," the deputy inspector said. "We didn't get it."

"I suppose the fire did. Anyway, Farwell had plenty of opportunity to know something about me and what better alibi witness than someone he considered a cop? But before he could call anyone he had things to do. Fortunately or unfortunately, depending upon your viewpoint, he had several hours in which to operate."

"Go on, I'm with you."

"All right. Besides directing suspicion away from himself, he must have thought it an excellent idea to turn it upon someone else—someone with a none-too-savory reputation, like Solly Spanish. He needed some article that would turn attention there or at least add to the general confusion. Leaving the house, he dropped by there and probably stole the first thing he could get hold of which was the pillow with the name on it. If Irma Nelson hadn't been afraid that Solly was guilty and lied about it you might have cleaned the whole thing up then."

"That's the story of my life," O'Callahan said. "People lying when the truth would make things so easy."

"Now then," McGann said. "All he needed was a dark theatrical wig. Everything else was here. He picked one up and came back here. Having the pick of Ronnie's wardrobe, he outfitted himself exactly as Tompkins was dressed, borrowing his diamond ring."

"How about that shot you heard? A blank?"

"Yes. The automatic used in the murder had, of course, thrown out the shell. All Farwell had to do was take the powder and wadding from one of the extra cartridges in the box and reload it. That's your missing cartridge. You'll probably find it in a washbowl trap."

"Then he called you."

"The whole thing nearly collapsed again when Wexton came to the door. Just why Ronnie had left that message for Wexton earlier in the day we'll never know. He may have wanted to alert him to his pending elopement with Miss Jones here." He looked down at Chary, who was examining her hands. "Farwell had no desire to try his disguise on anyone who knew Tompkins well, so after one peek from the window he declined to answer the door."

"Then you came along."

"Wexton went away and I came along, as you say. Farwell had his act nicely arranged. Pretending to be Ronnie, he showed me the art gallery and gave me a big buildup in here. He told me that 'Farwell' was drunk and asleep upstairs and all the rest as I described to you on the night of the murder.

"He had to work fast after sending me out to talk with 'Farwell' but split-second timing came natural to a radio actor, I presume." McGann walked over to Wexton who was reclining on one elbow. He said, "You're dead, lie down." Again he seized him under the arms, now pulling him to the middle of the room.

"This time he turned the body over on its back so that external bleeding would start. He put the ring back on Tompkins' finger and slipped the pillow under his head. Then all he had to do was to slide the murder gun under the drape, open the window and put his prepared blank on one of the burning logs."

"And get upstairs—"

"In a hurry. Using this back staircase he could get into the room without going into the front hall. I probably was already kicking on the door. He ripped off the wig and the borrowed tuxedo, took a mouthful of whiskey and stuck his head in the washbowl. His special hurry was to let me into the room before the fire exploded that shell downstairs. Splashing a little water into his eyes, plus the whiskey breath, completed the drunk act. We were talking when the blank went off. As he had hoped, the force knocked it back onto the floor. You know the rest." McGann turned to Farwell. "Any corrections?"

Perspiration stood on the pasty cheeks. A sickly smile touched the loose mouth. "You gotta admit it was good," Farwell said.

"Oh, I do," McGann said. "But only extraordinary luck got you through. I didn't touch the gun or I would have found it cold. The heat of that staircase kept the body from cooling off too quickly and warning the medical examiner's assistant."

Farwell straightened with an actor's response to a leading role. "That wasn't luck," he said. "I thought of everything—"

"Everything except Shirley Stanton's reaction. You didn't figure she'd chance losing her drug contact and tell her suspicions."

The smile faded and the disc jockey shivered. "She's better off. Once this stuff gets you, you're better off dead."

Wexton said, "I warn you. Either I get up now or I go to sleep."

"All right." McGann pulled him to his feet, again faced O'Callahan. "Mr. Farwell kept getting in deeper and his panic increased. He gave Shirley Stanton an overdose of morphine in a cup of coffee but nobody seriously considered suicide and the investigation was merely intensified."

McGann told of exploring the old house that preceding night, and of finding the soiled dress shirt in the hamper. "There had been other indications of a very fast deal but the shirt didn't fit in with anything I knew then. Now we know that Farwell had had time to discard it and put the tuxedo away while I was down here waiting for police. Maybe he didn't notice that he had gotten blood on it while handling Tompkins' body. Or perhaps he just had no chance to destroy it. At any rate, he probably expected it to be overlooked in the general linen."

Wexton asked, "What was all this hoopla about Chary?"

"Farwell's last attempt to get out from under," McGann said. "He must have started work on it early Monday after he saw that Stanton's death wouldn't save him. But if Chary could telephone someone, make what appeared to be a confession and then be found dead, the investigation might well be closed."

He looked at her soberly. "Just how he got her here this morning she'll have to tell us herself but it wasn't hard to guess how the telephone call was worked."

Walking over to Tompkins' record player, McGann lifted the lid. There was a record on the turntable. "I can't claim that I detected the difference between Tompkins' real voice and the one Farwell handed me here, especially on a machine, right off. But there was enough of a hunch to make me want to hear it again.

"I went looking for it and was doubly suspicious to learn that Farwell also had asked for it 'for his collection.' Luckily, Pearson intercepted and tried to steal it or it would have been very accidentally broken as soon as Farwell got it. Anyway, he must have become desperate and resolved to go after Chary at the first opportunity. This is what I heard on the phone."

McGann started the machine and lowered the needle. There was a moment's pause and then Chary spoke. "I'm sorry," she said. "You won't see me again." She began to weep. "It will be better this way. I don't know what happened to me . . . really I don't . . ."

Chary was watching the machine with parted lips. McGann turned the volume up and she winced.

"Just far away," the machine said. ". . . sometimes things happen . . . and people do things they never dreamed they would . . . or could . . ." He let it run to the last "goodbye."

She laid her palm against her cheek. "What I did to those plays," she said.

"I thought your performance unusually vivid," McGann said. O'Callahan looked thoroughly puzzled. "Bits from things Chary did on the radio," McGann explained. "They keep master transcriptions of all programs, mostly to guard against libel suits, and it was easy for Farwell, on the inside, to get playbacks and re-press what he wanted yesterday. Right, Frazier?"

"I'm tuning out on you," Farwell sneered. "This is longer than my commercials."

McGann shrugged. "I learned at the radio station early today that Farwell was an accomplished mimic. When I got a chance to study the Tompkins' record—and Dink confirmed that it was Ronnie's true voice—I knew that I had never spoken to Tompkins in this room. A good imitator was next choice.

"Then when I heard Chary's lines coming over the phone, was unable to break in and began to recognize some of them from plays she said she'd broadcast, I realized how it was being done. This place seemed by far the most logical source if Farwell was to cast her as a remorse-ridden suicide."

"That right, Miss?" O'Callahan asked.

She nodded, her eyes immense in a pallid face. "Can I go now?" O'Callahan stood up and held out his hand to McGann.

"You did very well, my boy," he said magnanimously. "It would have taken us at least another twelve hours."

"Awfully kind," McGann murmured. He inclined his head toward Wexton. "Is Joe Pulitzer here all clear with the department?"

"Certainly, certainly!" A fresh smile went with the booming voice. "I can't stay mad at a little journalistic enterprise. I was a newspaperman myself once, you know."

"Really?"

"Absolutely. Sold ads for the *Bronx Home News* in the summer of 1907. I guess it stays in the blood." He beamed at Wexton. "We didn't see anything in that desk anyway, did we?"

"Nooo," Wexton said. "Not a thing."

O'Callahan waved a big paw at the man in blue. "Okay, Charlie, give your friend a hand there."

Chary had drawn away but she let McGann take her by the elbow. He said, "How about a cup of coffee?"

Her voice was like a small girl's. "I want to go home."

"All right. I'll drive you home and we'll pick up something on the way."

"Deal me in," Wexton said. "I'm not so pretty but I'm a hero."

24
LAST ADD MURDER

Sunlight stabbed at their eyes as they emerged. Shutters clicked and a little group of men and women surged forward. One called, "C'mon, Wexton, you rat, how about a statement?"

"Mother, I've dreamed of this," Wexton said. His eyes gleamed above their brown bags. "Sorry, gentlemen. No comment."

They were still hooting as the convertible pulled away. McGann let the top slide back and they drank in the sun-washed breeze. Central Park slipped past, cool and quiet. McGann wound along the drives leisurely, letting their taut nerves soften. Occasionally he glanced down at Chary, between them in the front seat. She seemed more relaxed but she would not meet his gaze.

He swung out into the West Seventies and eased to the curb near a restaurant, looking at Wexton expectantly. The reporter bristled. "You mean I'm back to a busboy again?" he demanded. "The pride of the Alamo?"

"Three coffees to go," McGann said firmly, "and no one will ever know that you came through that window backwards."

Wexton sighed and squirmed out. "Sees all, knows all, tells all. May you always have somebody to back over a windowsill in your trying moments."

They drank the hot coffee from cardboard containers and Wexton mused happily over the morning finals. The *Blade* headline was the biggest and blackest since the last Armistice. He gloated over the opposition. "There's a hot lead story," he said. "Students riot in Bolivia."

"Where do you want to go?" McGann asked.

Wexton decided to drop by the office to accept the plaudits of the multitude. They left him on the sidewalk there. McGann shook hands and Chary kissed him on the cheek. "My backward hero," she said.

"It was nothing. Any time."

As soon as they pulled away, she said, "I suppose you think I'm an awful fool."

McGann said, "Umm."

"It was just that you made me so damned mad—as if you took me out like a—a suspect, after you got through with Irma and that Rogers woman." Another thought seemed to strike her. "I suppose your hat will be dry by cocktail time."

"No," McGann said. "She can have it as a permanent trophy now. Is that why you checked out of the hotel in such a hurry before?"

"Partly. It was hard to believe that you were so solicitous about my welfare." Her lips relaxed in a tentative smile. "And the way you reacted to Frazier—well . . ."

He grinned. "So you went back to the studio to get my goat? Frazier must have thought all hell was on his side when you walked in."

"I don't know how I ever fell for the line he handed out. He said he had a key copied from Shirley's long ago for emergencies and that we could go over there and solve the whole thing. We'd fix the room just like it was the night of the murder and figure it out."

"Gosh," McGann said. He nosed across Broadway and headed for Ninth Avenue. "That would certainly have beaten my time hands down."

"The next thing I knew was when that horrible cloth was on my face." She shuddered. "He's terribly strong."

"Not really," McGann said. "Narcotics and desperation for his own life stepped him up."

Ninth Avenue was coming to life. Merchants bustled around produce stands, dustmops waggled from windows and an occasional comforter was flung over a fire-escape railing. Youngsters hurried along with morning breakfast rolls.

McGann eyed the scene speculatively. "This is as good as Third Avenue anytime," he said. "You may marry a Rockefeller yet."

"I couldn't bear it. Can you imagine a wash with all that horrible oil on the shirts every week? Nothing harder to get out."

"Unless it's lipstick?"

"Umm." She pointed ahead. "Fourth from the corner. It's more picturesque in the daytime, don't you think?"

McGann pulled over. He walked around and opened the door. She held her gloves and her hand was cool in his as he helped her out. "Thank you for everything," she said. "Give my best to Irma, won't you?"

"She and Solly will probably get married as soon as they see the papers." He watched the dark lashes come up. "Absolutely. I gave them my blessing last night."

"Oh."

"If there's anything else I can do—?"

"No . . . oh, yes." She opened her purse and found a key. "I left that overnight case in a locker at Grand Central. I won't need anything in it until this evening. Would you?" She was smiling. McGann decided it was prettier than Ronnie Tompkins' picture.

"Would I?" McGann took the key. "I wish you had checked it in the lion's cage at the zoo," he said. "I'd pick it up just before feeding time."

ABOUT THE AUTHOR

Fred Dickenson (1909-1986) was a new police reporter on Chicago's North Side when gangsters on his beat mowed down seven members of the "Bugs" Moran mob in the spectacular St. Valentine's Day massacre, providing a flying start for a newspaperman even in the Windy City's prohibition era. The next few years were a blend of exploding pineapples and expiring racketeers, during which the author also covered the Criminal Court beat as an editorial bat-boy for the late Hildy Johnson of Front Page fame. Switching from Chicago to Los Angeles newspapers merely meant a chronicling change from mobsters to murderesses, specifically Winnie Ruth Judd, who stuffed two chums into a trunk and expressed them to the City of Angels. In Oklahoma, Dickenson accepted a commission as a reserve deputy sheriff but successfully avoided forays into the Cookson Hills in search of "Pretty Boy" Floyd. With the same determination, he trailed John Dillinger through Wisconsin. "Once I almost caught up with him in Milwaukee," Dickenson says. "After that, I was more careful." The author, on the Newark, N.J., death watch for Arthur ("Dutch Schultz") Flegenheimer, also noted the finish of the last beer baron. After a further stint in Washington, D.C., Dickenson finally settled in New York City with his wife, a former airline stewardess, and three blonde daughters, working as an associate editor with King Features Syndicate, and a writer of mystery stories both real and fancied. He wrote the *Rip Kirby* comic strip from 1952 to 1985.

COACHWHIP PUBLICATIONS
CoachwhipBooks.com

THE
SARA ELIZABETH
MASON
MYSTERIES

MURDER RENTS A ROOM

THE CRIMSON FEATHER

COACHWHIP PUBLICATIONS
CoachwhipBooks.com

THE
SARA ELIZABETH
MASON
MYSTERIES

THE HOUSE THAT HATE BUILT

>>>> <<<<

THE WHIP

COACHWHIP PUBLICATIONS
CoachwhipBooks.com

THE
RUMBLE
MURDERS

Henry Ware Eliot, Jr.

COACHWHIP PUBLICATIONS
CoachwhipBooks.com

ANONYMOUS FOOTSTEPS | JOHN. M. O'CONNOR

COACHWHIP PUBLICATIONS
COACHWHIPBOOKS.COM

A JUDGE MASSIE MYSTERY

THE CORPSE IS INDIGNANT

DOUGLAS STAPLETON
and HELEN A. CAREY

COACHWHIP PUBLICATIONS
COACHWHIPBOOKS.COM

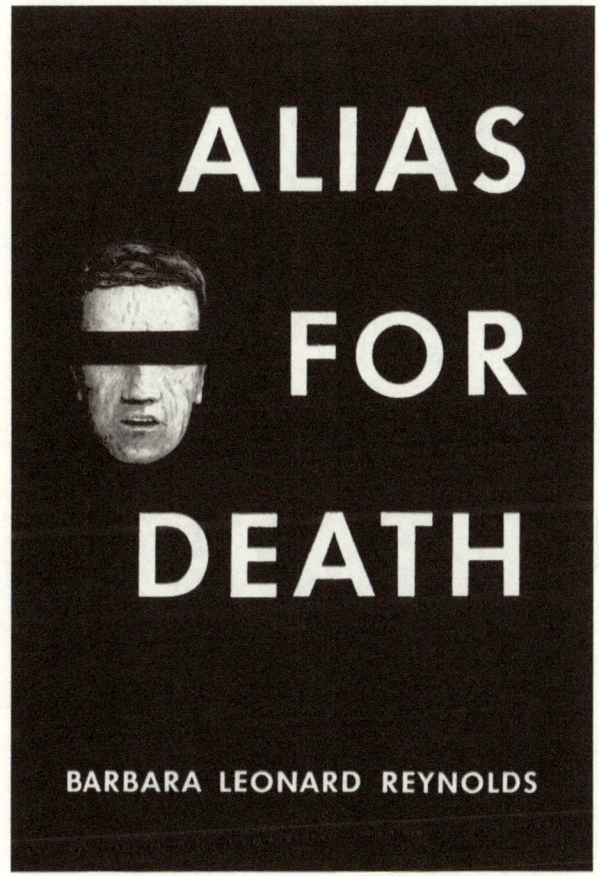

COACHWHIP PUBLICATIONS
CoachwhipBooks.com

COACHWHIP PUBLICATIONS
CoachwhipBooks.com